Hot Greek Docs

They're supersexy and *they're single—
but not for much longer!*

Theo, Deakin, Ares and Christos have vowed
never to surrender their freedom by putting a ring
on it—but who'd have thought it would literally
take an earthquake to change their minds?

While these gorgeous Greeks are busy saving
the islanders of Mythelios after the quake,
they can't avoid the four equally dedicated women
who are right by their sides…day *and* night!

Find out what happens in:

One Night with Dr. Nikolaides by Annie O'Neil
Tempted by Dr. Patera by Tina Beckett

Available now!

Back in Dr. Xenakis' Arms by Amalie Berlin
A Date with Dr. Moustakas by Amy Ruttan

Available July 2018!

Dear Reader,

Home. For many people that word conjures up images of family gatherings, of children playing and of growing into adulthood. It's a place we like to revisit from time to time, either physically or in our memories. But for Deakin Patera, the small Greek island that was his childhood home is a place he'd rather avoid. Only, fate, his trust fund and a terrible earthquake have other ideas.

Thank you for joining Deakin and beautiful psychiatrist Leanora Risi as they explore the meanings of *home* and *family*, and how the heartache each of them has gone through has changed the way they view those things. And maybe, just maybe, they'll discover something that can transcend the pain and grief they've endured.

I hope you enjoy reading about this very special couple as much as I've loved writing their story!

Love,

Tina Beckett

TEMPTED BY
DR. PATERA

———

TINA BECKETT

HARLEQUIN® MEDICAL ROMANCE™

Recycling programs
for this product may
not exist in your area.

ISBN-13: 978-1-335-66355-9

Tempted by Dr. Patera

First North American Publication 2018

Printed in U.S.A.

To my family. You *are* my home.

PROLOGUE

THE IMAGES FLASHING across the television screen were…horrific.

Deakin Patera's gut became a tight ball of fear as he strained to make out the words. He couldn't hear the newscaster's voice over the noise in the bar, but he knew that landscape—that shoreline—by heart. And the text crawling along the bottom of the screen told snippets of the story: *Eight point one earthquake rocks Greek island. Hundreds injured. Death toll not yet available. A few still missing.*

Who?

Hell! Who?

Pulling out his phone, he checked for text messages. He had one from his aunt.

Safe for now. Will advise about aftershocks. No damage on the house, thank God. Where are you?

No damage on the house. Unlike that other time. His palm scrubbed over the rough skin on the side of his neck, even though that particular damage had faded long ago.

He typed a quick message back.

Glad you're safe. I'm in Africa on medical mission. Any word from the others?

She would know who he was talking about. His best friends from childhood. They had all partnered together to open a much-needed clinic on their home island—just as their parents had all partnered together to found Mopaxeni Shipping, the company that had made them all rich.

Deakin rarely saw the clinic nowadays, but Theo kept him apprised of how it was doing. Their joint trust funds paid the bulk of the expenses, but a crisis like this one was going to stretch its finances to breaking point.

He kept half an eye on the reports as he scrolled through the contacts on his phone.

There were worries over tsunamis rolling in from the sea. His aunt hadn't said anything about that, and nor had she texted back about his friends.

He sent off another question.

Tsunamis?

Within seconds he had a reply.

So far, no, thank God. But we're on high ground. Should be okay. I have a message out to Theo. Chris and Ares aren't on the island. Haven't heard of damage to the clinic. The airstrip is a wreck, though. No flights in or out at the moment.

No flights. Well, at least they were able to get messages in and out—although that could change at any moment as more and more people tried to get a hold of loved ones.

His aunt hadn't heard from Theo. Where was he?

Even as he thought it, his phone began to vibrate in his hand. The readout was exactly what he wanted to see.

Thank God!

He shot off a final text to his aunt.

Will write more soon.

Then he answered the call.

"Theo, glad to hear from you."

"Don't be glad. Not yet. You've heard?"

Was his friend injured? The clinic decimated?

"I'm just seeing the news. Is it as bad as it looks?"

"If you mean does the island look like it's been through a meat grinder…almost. Where are you?"

The same question his aunt had asked.

"Africa. I still have a bit more than a month left on my contract."

"Find a way to get out of it, then. Mythelios needs you."

"No, it doesn't. It's done fine without me—*better* without me."

A sigh came over the phone. "Stop with the tired excuses, already. That was ages ago. Everyone who matters has already forgotten."

His parents were dead, so *they* certainly had. But everyone?

"*I* haven't forgotten. And I bet if you asked Ville neither has he."

He scrubbed a hand over his neck once again. Even without the obvious reminders looking back at him in the mirror he would never be able to erase those images from his head. Of his best friend's grin right before the world exploded before his eyes.

"Ville's family moved off the island ten years ago. Besides, it doesn't matter."

Before he had time to draw enough breath to throw another excuse at his friend Theo brushed it aside with a sharp expletive.

"No buts, Deak. We've had this argument before. Mythelios is suffering. So put aside your self-pity for once. It's time for you to do the right thing. Come home. The sooner, the better."

CHAPTER ONE

THE CRUSH OF people in the inner sanctum of the clinic made Leanora Risi wince. Just over a month since the earthquake and the flow of those emotionally and physically wounded had not completely abated.

Many were drawn to the steady presence of the clinic and its outside garden. It had gotten so it was hard for her to find a quiet corner in which to hear from those who were still having problems dealing with the after-effects. She was well past the end of her vacation and her savings were slowly dwindling. She was going to have to make a decision about whether to leave or not…soon.

But not right now.

A man with dark shaggy hair and a jaw shadowed with what had to be a three-week growth of whiskers made his way to the front desk. There was an exhaustion about him that went beyond physical tiredness. It was in the way his eyes shifted slowly from one person to the next. He greeted several of them, shaking their hands, but it was a rapid clasp and release. Not the hearty greeting most of the islanders gave each other.

He reached the desk, but didn't take the pen to sign in. Instead he flipped over the top sheet with his right hand and started studying the entries.

An internal alarm went off inside her. While it wasn't against the rules for patients to glance at the list of other patients to see how long the wait would be—at least she didn't think it was—the way he was acting was odd, making her gut tighten.

The number of patients they'd had right after the earthquake was staggering, and they had ended up just stacking new sheets on top of the old ones, since they hadn't had time to sit down and collate the data and put the sign-in times on charts yet. Even though things had evened out quite a bit, there were still things they hadn't completely caught up with.

When those long fingers flicked another sheet over, it was Lea's signal to move. Murmuring an apology as she accidentally brushed shoulders with an older woman, she hurried forward, arriving beside the man and firmly placing her hand on the first couple of sheets, trapping his beneath them.

"Can I help you with something?"

His gaze swiveled from the stack of papers to her face. Up went dark brows, a hint of irritation marring his rugged features. "You can let me see how many patients have been treated today."

That inner alarm became less certain. Those low growled words didn't sound apologetic. At all. No sign of the nosy-neighbor-caught-with-binoculars-up-to-his-eyes syndrome. Instead he acted as if he had a right to look at those pages. But she didn't recognize him. She would have remembered those high cheekbones, that bump in an otherwise straight nose.

Although…wasn't there…?

What?

Despite the whiskers, his strong jaw was clearly visible. This was a man who wasn't easily deterred from something he wanted. She just wasn't sure what that something was.

She blinked to bring the room back into focus. Still filled with people. A few of them were on the list, waiting to be seen, but many just needed the solid presence of the clinic to ground them.

She lifted her hand from the papers, although she probably shouldn't. He still hadn't explained who he was.

"May I ask what you're looking for, specifically?"

"I believe I already explained that, Ms….?"

Her chin tilted. "It's Dr. Dr. Risi."

"I wasn't aware the clinic had hired a new doctor." His voice downshifted, becoming a little less gruff. "Where is Petra?"

"Petra's mom hasn't felt well since the earthquake. She's been going home during her lunch break to check on her."

How did he know the clinic receptionist's name? Although most of the islanders in this area seemed to know each other.

And now he was flipping through those patient sheets once again. "I don't see a list of symptoms or injuries."

"There isn't one. Things got too chaotic, trying to separate them out, so we just did triage, taking the critical patients first. We put the ones who were stable but needed a specialist in a secondary waiting area in the Serenity Gardens."

Facing the ocean, the courtyard led to a spacious garden that faced the sea. Lea's tiny treatment area had been carved out of a dead-end path, shielded on two sides by vine-covered trellises.

It was the perfect place for her to see patients who needed to work through what they'd experienced during the quake. It was wonderful, and restful, and despite the tragedy she loved what she was doing there. More than she'd ever dreamed possible.

The people in the waiting area weren't the only ones who needed to be grounded. She'd come to Greece to do just that. And had ended up on the island just as the quake hit. She'd stayed to help.

Her attention came back with a bump when the man in front of her made a slight scoffing noise.

"What?"

"Nothing."

It was then that she realized she still didn't know who he was. He could be a psychiatric patient for all she knew. "Do you need to leave a message for Petra?"

He frowned. "Is Theo—Dr. Nikolaides—back yet?"

Theo had just gotten engaged. His whirlwind romance with Cailey had been a bright spot for the clinic, and probably one of the reasons why there were more people than normal here. It was as if folks wanted to catch a glimpse of the couple—live vicariously through those who had been able to find happiness in the midst of tragedy. Cailey was also nearly two months pregnant, and the baby had become a symbol of hope.

"He's taking a much-needed personal day. Did you have a consultation scheduled with him?"

Maybe he actually *was* a patient.

"Not exactly." One side of his mouth went up in a half-smile that sent her pulse tripping over itself. "He called me. Basically said I was an emotionless so-and-so if I didn't come home as soon as I could."

Home…

Home?

Then she swallowed—hard—an awful suspicion crashing like a boulder in the pit of her stomach. "You *live* here?"

His smile widened and he let the papers fall back into place as he turned toward her. "I don't live *in* the clinic, if that's what you mean."

"No, I don't mean that, I just…" She was at a loss for words—which was unusual, since talking was what she was paid to do. What she loved to do. No, it wasn't the words. It was the listening…the empathizing…the *helping* that she loved.

Although she couldn't help everyone.

Her eyes closed as a shot of pain punched through her chest.

No, don't think about that. Not now.

Something touched her hand. "Hey. Are you okay?"

"Yes." She forced herself to smile. "I'm just tired. And I forgot to ask who you are."

"Of course. Sorry, I just always assume that everyone knows who I am." Something dark slithered through his brown eyes. Then it was gone again as quickly as it had come. "I'm Deakin Patera. I'm one of the four founding partners of the clinic."

Ack!

God, she should have realized. Theo had said Dr. Patera was due to arrive in the next couple of days. She just hadn't expected someone who looked like he'd stepped straight off the cover of a wilderness backpacking magazine. He could have told her who he was sooner. Emphasized his medical title like she had.

She wasn't even sure why she'd done that. Maybe because she'd expected him to talk down to her like a few colleagues had over the years. But those people had been few and far between.

"I'm sorry. I didn't recognize you."

He dragged a hand through his hair. "It's

okay. It's been a long flight, and it's not like our portraits are on the walls or anything. Thank God."

What an odd thing to say. She smiled. "Maybe they should be. Your reputations seem to be known far and wide."

The softness to his eyes disappeared. "I'm sure they are."

Those four words might have come across as arrogant boasting if not for the strange tone in which they were said. It was as if he despised that fact.

"I don't understand."

"It's nothing." His glance turned to the occupants of the room. "Where do we begin?"

The words to a famous old musical song came to mind, but there was no way she was breaking into song. Not around *this* particular man. Besides she couldn't compete with the likes of Julie Andrews.

"A lot of these people are just meeting friends and family here." She nodded at the foursome who were even now passing through the wooden and glass doors off to the left. "The clinic seems to have become almost as much of a meeting place as Stavros's *taverna*. And, since the bar is within walking distance, it makes it ideal."

With its traditional white stucco exterior

and well-manicured gardens to the side of it, the clinic was a beautiful building, combining old-world charm with all the modern amenities of a medical facility. The Serenity Gardens boasted many nooks and crannies, ideal for intimate conversations, and benches were sprinkled along a curving walkway which was wide enough for wheelchairs and yet rustic enough to invite exploring. A white sea wall and a boat dock were newer additions.

"I can see that. Theo always did want this place to be more than just a medical clinic. Hence the so-called Tranquility Gardens."

"They're called the *Serenity* Gardens, and it doesn't sound like you approve of the addition."

He shrugged, his dark shirt pulling tight over muscular shoulders. Shoulders her eyes had no business lingering on. She hauled her attention back to his face.

"It's not that I disapprove," he said. "I just don't believe a manufactured place can bring tranquility. *Serenity*," he corrected. His smile came back, although the left side of his mouth didn't quite lift as high as the other. "Although Theo is convinced it can."

"I think it can as well. It's where I see most of my patients."

"How does that work? Did Theo put an exam room out there?"

The image of a hospital bed nestled between the flower pots made her smile back. "No. Not yet, anyway. I use the exam rooms, obviously, for physical investigation, but the garden is much more conducive to talking things through."

"Things? Such as unfavorable diagnoses?"

"Not exactly. I guess this is where I should say that I'm a psychiatrist." She held up her hands. "No couch jokes, please."

His head jerked back, a muscle in his jaw twitching for a second before going still. "Couch jokes are the farthest thing from my mind at the moment. Theo hired you?"

She bit her lip. Maybe the Serenity Gardens wasn't the only thing Dr. Patera would disapprove of. "I just happened to be on the island when the earthquake hit. I stayed to help. It's on a volunteer basis at the moment."

"The quake happened over a month ago. What about your own practice?"

It was her turn to shrug. "I'd already given notice at my hospital, so I'm kind of between jobs."

"And where was that? In Athens?"

Ah, he thought she actually lived in *Greece*. One of the perks of having parents who had immigrated to Canada from Greece when she was a kid was that she was bilingual. The fact that he hadn't heard any trace of an accent made her happy. As did the ease with which the islanders seemed to have accepted her.

"No, I lived in Canada. Toronto."

"Your family is Greek, though."

It wasn't a question. "Yes. They moved there when I was young."

Someone came up on his right and said something to him. Dr. Patera turned his head to give the man his attention and Lea's breath stalled in her lungs at what that shift of position revealed.

Scars. Big ones.

Wickedly thick, they began at the lower half of his strong square jaw and formed twin streams that coursed down the side of his neck, disappearing beneath the collar of his shirt. Continuing on to those shoulders she'd just been admiring? Probably. The scars were paler than the rest of his skin. So they were old.

How old?

God. Those wounds must have been agonizing when they were fresh. Debriding. Skin grafts. Therapy to allow for movement. All part of third-degree burn treatment.

What had caused them? An explosive device? Some kind of caustic agent? Maybe he'd been in the military or something. She had a feeling that what she'd thought was an attractive lopsidedness to his smile might be due to the contracture of skin and muscle drawing everything down. Her gaze traveled to his chest. How many more scars were hidden beneath his clothes?

Her mind tossed an image of a very naked Dr. Patera at her—one who aimed that scrumptious crooked smile right at her and sent her brain into overdrive. She swallowed hard, feeling a weird shifting sensation burrowing through her midsection. Her teeth dug into her bottom lip.

Oh, Lord, what was once seen could not be unseen.

Except she hadn't *really* seen him naked. She'd just—

His attention shifted back to her with a suddenness she hadn't expected. She released her lip in a hurry, but it was too late. She knew it the second his eyes flickered to her mouth and back up.

She'd seen them. His damned scars.

He gave an inner grimace. They were kind of obvious. His tendency to keep his right profile to a person was ingrained from years of trying to keep the damage to his skin out of sight. Hidden, but not forgotten.

Along with his sense of shame?

Probably. The two things seemed to go hand in hand. It was one of the things that had kept him from wanting to come back to the island. Almost every person on Mythelios knew what he'd done. Or at least they thought they did.

Except Dr. Risi, here. And now even *she* had seen the evidence—she just didn't know the reason for it.

He wasn't even sure why he'd participated in the founding of this clinic. He'd wanted to leave after medical school and never come back. And for the most part he'd done exactly that. But his three best friends in the world had been determined to take their parents' tarnished legacies and turn them into something good. And as long as he could give his input from a distance he was good with that. His traveling did the trick for the most part. He was able to give his nods of approval from afar, except when they absolutely needed his physical presence.

Like now.

If he'd expected to see a quick show of pity on this new doctor's face, though, he was sorely disappointed. She met his gaze with steady green eyes that gave nothing away.

That was probably the psychiatrist in her. She was trained to listen without judging. Not to seem shocked or horrified, no matter how ugly the story. Or how hideous the outward appearance.

His dad—after a rare crack had appeared in his chilly demeanor—had once sent him to a shrink in Athens, six months after the accident. But Deakin, his scars still fresh and painful, had refused to say anything. After four sessions of sitting there in sullen silence they'd given up. All of them—including the psychiatrist.

He tried to recall what Lea had been talking about moments earlier, working to forget the way those white teeth had captured that full bottom lip in a way that was far too sexy for a psychiatrist.

He switched to English so those around would be less likely to understand them if she tried to ask about his scars. "So, what part of Greece were your parents from?"

"Athens—like you thought. My dad was a welder and went to Canada to help with the building of one of the Orthodox churches. He ended up staying." She sent a lock of long dark hair spinning over her shoulder with a flick of her wrist. "He sent for me and my mom a few months later, and we went, sight unseen. But we love it there now."

The switch in language hadn't thrown her for a loop. In fact her English was as flawless as her Greek. He knew himself well enough to know that his Greek accent was still fairly strong, even after years of speaking English in other countries.

"You don't ever get homesick for Greece?"

"Not really. I was a kid when things changed."

That he understood. He didn't get homesick either. And he'd also been a kid when things had changed. Only, unlike for her, the change hadn't been a good one for him.

She went on. "Besides, you can find Greeks on almost every street corner."

"You can, indeed." Deakin had found pockets of Greek communities almost everywhere he'd gone. "Well, shall we get started? Are you only seeing patients who need counseling?"

"No, we've been kind of short-staffed, as you can imagine, so I've been helping wherever I can. The immediate injuries from the quake have been taken care of, but there are still issues—broken bones, lacerations that have become infected… Burns. But I *have* been seeing patients who are struggling to cope with the after effects of the earthquake.

It's what I specialize in. People dealing with PTSD."

He tried to ignore the way she'd hesitated before saying the word "burns."

"PTSD from time served in the military?"

"No, civilian for the most part. Trauma comes in many forms."

Yes, it did. He wasn't sure if she was subtly trying to dig into his past struggles, but he wasn't going to take any chances. He didn't need someone probing where they didn't belong.

Time to get to work.

Just then Petra came back from wherever she'd been and glanced his way. She did a double-take, her eyes widening.

"Deakin!"

She rushed through the door to the waiting room and grabbed him in a strong, matronly embrace.

Her graying locks were scraped back into a bun and dark-rimmed glasses were pushed on top of her head. The combination gave her a no-nonsense appearance. One that was well-deserved. She could be formidable when she wanted to be.

"It's about time you came home."

He stiffened at that word. This wasn't his

home. Not anymore. But at least her presence took Dr. Risi's attention off him.

"I'm sure you're keeping the clinic running like a well-oiled machine."

She dropped her glasses onto her nose and peered at him over the top of them. "It's not easy, let me tell you."

"I'm sure. Did Chris or Ares make it home yet?"

"No. Not yet. But I'm hopeful you will all be reunited soon. It's been too long."

"Yes, it has."

While he didn't miss the island, he did miss his friends.

"So, Theo has been handling the crisis alone?" He'd thought maybe the others would have made it back sooner than him.

"Well, he has Cailey now. She's been a huge help. And Lea has been *aprosdókito kaló*. She's very organized. And beautiful, don't you think?"

Color bloomed in the psychiatrist's face. Petra had called the doctor a godsend. And beautiful.

And Petra was right. She was very attractive. Dark-lashed eyes gleamed with purpose beneath arched brows. And with each upward curve of her lips high cheekbones appeared.

And yet there was something lurking just

beneath the surface. He'd caught glimpses of it when she'd talked about PTSD. Did her patients' pain affect her on a personal level? He knew from experience that as much as you tried to maintain an emotional distance there were some patients who touched something inside you.

His own throat tightened whenever he was called on to treat a child who'd suffered horrific burns or who had lost limbs from incendiary devices or from IEDs. It was why he did what he did.

"I think you've embarrassed Dr. Risi, Petra."

"It's okay. I'm fine. And please call me Lea. We all tend to be informal around here."

The way she said that make him take a closer look at her. She didn't *sound* fine. Did she think the older woman was trying to set them up somehow? Well, she needn't worry. He wasn't about to start a romance with anyone—especially not someone with ties to this island.

But she didn't have ties—had said she didn't get homesick for Greece. She was a temporary visitor, that was all. She wasn't staying on the island for long.

The image of those teeth gripping that lip in a tight embrace sashayed across the backs of his eyelids, playing peekaboo with a neglected part of his anatomy. He could think of a way to make her do that all over again. For very different reasons.

He stopped that thought in its tracks. *Not happening.* She could be leaving tomorrow for all he knew.

His job didn't lend itself to relationships. And that suited him just fine. Theo might have found true love, but that was something Deakin neither wanted nor needed. Because relationships meant exposing the worst of yourself to someone else.

Lea pushed that errant strand of hair over her shoulder once again and glanced out over the waiting room, which was gradually clearing out.

"It may not look that way, but this is one of our slower times." She looked at the sign-in sheet. "It'll stay that way until after lunch."

Deakin was having a hard time understanding why exactly he was even here. Could he fly out before Theo realized he had arrived?

"Are you still seeing new injuries?"

"Some. There are a few buildings that still aren't stable. So we're seeing crush injuries. And with those unstable buildings come gas lines and electric wires, so there's a chance of electrocution and burns—"

She was still talking, but that last word was

all he heard in that moment. It was the second time she'd said it.

Deakin's father had replaced his boat. It was right there in the rebuilt boathouse. Leaving it to Deakin in his will had seemed like the ultimate slap in the face, but since they'd left everything else to him as well it probably hadn't been meant like that. But Deakin had kept it, taking that vessel out for a spin every time he came home—which wasn't often. But the guests that booked his home were granted full use of the grounds—including his Jeep and the boat.

"Hello?" Lea snapped her fingers in front of his face. "Are you okay?"

He frowned, hating being caught thinking about his past. "I'm fine. I'm just dealing with a serious case of jet lag. I need a shave and a shower."

"You must be exhausted. Did you come straight here after landing on the mainland?"

"Yes, but I'm fine." He wasn't, but it had nothing to do with being tired.

There was no way he was going to share any of that with her. *Temporary visitor, remember?*

Petra interrupted. "I talked to your aunt this morning. She was sure you were arriving today and said to send you straight over to the house. She's put a moussaka in the fridge for you."

His Aunt Cecilia was in charge of renting out his parents' house and his cottage to tourists. It seemed better than letting them sit empty and untended.

"Great." He glanced at the wall behind the reception desk, frowning when something caught his eye.

Dammit. What was *that* doing there?

He shook his head and tried to continue his thought. "Where did you end up staying?" he asked Lea.

"At a private cottage a few miles from here."

Petra laughed. "A few miles from here in *that* direction." Her hand waved a few times in the air before pointing to the west.

There probably weren't all that many bed and breakfasts operating right now. Not that the damage to the island was horrific, but he could pretty much guarantee that tourist income was down. Hadn't his aunt said that his house had been sitting vacant ever since the earthquake? Who wanted to vacation in a place torn apart by a natural disaster?

He couldn't think of anything on the west side of the island except for the expensive houses owned by people like his parents. Although… His house was in that general—

"*Whose* cottage?"

The receptionist smiled wickedly, while Lea looked thoroughly confused. "Theo, Cailey and your aunt figured it was the best place to house her, since the hotel she was staying at was damaged by the quake. So she's staying in the cottage, Deakin. *Your* cottage."

CHAPTER TWO

THIS WAS *DEAKIN'S* HOUSE?

She set a skillet on a burner to heat and gritted her teeth.

Why hadn't Theo told her? She'd assumed it was a relative's house or something. But the tiny white building behind the opulent house was perfect, and she loved staying there. The formal manicured grounds here made the Serenity Gardens look like something out of a dollhouse, although it was a gorgeous setting. The clinic's grounds were informal, while the house she was staying so close to screamed money. Even the boathouse had a tiny apartment over it.

She had never really stopped to think about who on the island could afford something like this. Theo had said he and his friends' parents had been part of something called Mopaxeni Shipping. They'd all been wealthy. She didn't know the whole story, and although the clinic was state of the art she had gotten the impression that they were only scraping by and looking for fundraisers.

Like that calendar over the desk in the main entryway at the clinic that boasted photos of twelve very hunky locals. Some of them were doctors, or employees of the clinic, and others were firefighters or involved in other lines of public service.

Deakin was somewhere in the main house at this very moment. It had been more than obvious that he wasn't happy with her being here. The look on his face when he'd realized exactly which cottage Petra was talking about had been priceless…and embarrassing. But unless she just wanted to leave the island there wasn't much she could do about it. And she was enjoying the work far too much to let Deakin's grumpiness drive her away.

The property was usually rented out when Deakin wasn't there, Theo had finally admitted when she'd called him and confronted him about the cottage. He hadn't been positive Deakin would come back when he'd offered it to her, and they'd needed her at the clinic. And for that to happen she'd needed someplace to sleep. It had been the only logical solution.

That didn't make it the most comfortable one now that Deakin was home. He'd claimed it didn't bother him to have her staying there, but his voice told another story.

Cracking an egg, she listened to the satisfying sizzle as it hit the heated oil, the earthy scent filling the air, making her mouth water.

She made her way to the refrigerator for some orange juice, pulling a small glass from a cupboard on the way. She could *do* this. From what she'd heard about Deakin, a plastic surgeon who specialized in treating burns victims, he didn't stay in one place for any length of time. He probably wouldn't be here for more than a week or two. As soon as he could Deakin would be on his way.

He didn't like the island. She wasn't sure how she knew that, but she did. It was in the way his eyes shifted from thing to thing, that ever-present frown on his face. Something here held bad vibes for him.

Maybe he'd been injured on the island?

It didn't matter.

She hadn't come to the island to speculate on its residents, past or present. She'd come here to escape.

No. Not to escape. To start over.

There was a difference. Starting over involved staying here on this earth, not——

Dammit.

A piercing shriek shattered her thoughts in

an instant, and her brain struggled to locate the source.

A smoke alarm, just behind her.

Why…?

Oh, no! Where there'd once been the satisfying crackle of a cooking egg there was now billowing smoke coming from the stovetop.

But that alarm…

God! Her ears!

The racket was huge and dramatic, with flashing strobe lights and a screeching caterwaul that reminded her of a seagull. Or maybe a million of them.

The hot oil wasn't actually on fire, thank heavens, so she rushed over and grabbed the pan. She was hurrying toward the sink with it just as the front door burst open.

Deakin appeared, stopping in his tracks as his eyes jerked from her face and landed on the pan, which was now safely under the tap.

He came over, putting both hands on the edge of the counter, his breath seesawing in and out. "What happened?"

She could barely make out the words over the alarm.

"I was trying to cook dinner, but…" She had to yell, her vocal cords straining. "Can you turn that thing off?"

He pulled a remote from the front pocket of

his chinos and aimed it toward the still blaring siren.

She sucked down a deep breath, her ears ringing in the sudden silence that followed. "Wow. Why didn't you just turn it off from the house? I think you got an industrial-sized alarm by mistake."

"No mistake. It's safer."

Her head tilted. *Safer?* Okay…whatever he said.

She gave a rueful gesture toward the skillet. "I'm sorry. I'll reimburse you, of course, if the pan is ruined."

"It's nothing. I thought the whole cottage was on fire."

It was then that she realized his upper lip was damp with perspiration and the tight lines running down the side of his face weren't from irritation but from something far worse. *Fear.*

Of what?

A smoke alarm went off, Lea, that's what.

He didn't want to lose his home to her stupidity. But she had never seen an alarm like that. Actually, when she looked closer she also saw ceiling sprinklers, jutting down at regular intervals.

"I guess I'm lucky the sprinklers didn't go off and give you water damage on top of everything else. I really am sorry."

He brushed aside her words. "It's nothing. I'm just glad you're okay. The sprinklers are set with a delay. If the alarm isn't shut down in ten minutes they engage, and then the fire department is notified."

There was a tense element to his voice, that made her take a closer look at the way he was perspiring.

A warning tingle started at the back of her head and traveled up over the top. She shut off the faucet. Maybe that was what those scars were from. A house fire. It would explain a lot. His apathy toward the island. His reluctance to return, according to Theo.

Bad memories?

If it had been the big house or this particular cottage, they had been rebuilt to perfection. They looked like they'd been standing on this rocky crag for the last century. Except for the boathouse. That was different from the main house and the cottage, even though it still blended in. It just seemed *newer*, somehow. But there was no way she was going to ask.

"I'm fine." She forced another smile. "Unfortunately my meal didn't fare quite as well."

"The smoke detector certainly didn't approve." A *beep-beep* accompanied a few more manipulations of the remote control. "There. I've reset it for you."

Just in case his panicked reaction *wasn't* all in her imagination, she decided to put his mind at ease. "Thanks. I'll stay far away from the stove tonight so I don't trip it again. Cold cuts it is."

He paused for a few long seconds before glancing at her, and sure enough his muscles seemed to relax all at once. "My aunt's moussaka is heating in the oven at the main house. There's more than enough if you want to share."

She tried to ignore the way her mouth watered. Moussaka was one of her favorite dishes. "Are you sure? I don't mind just making a sandwich."

If he was as uneasy about having her at the cottage as she thought he was, it was up to her to make sure her stay was as discreet as possible. Especially since there wasn't anywhere else for her to stay. At least not now. Maybe in another week or two something would open up and she could leave Deakin alone in his cottage on the hill.

"I'm sure. I was going to offer earlier, but I wasn't sure what your plans were."

"My plans are a bit charred now," she said, nodding at the sink. "You rent the house out, Theo said? The cottage as well?"

"Yes. Since my parents are both gone it's

the best way I can think of to keep them occupied, so their upkeep is not left completely up to my aunt."

His tight jaw said that his parents were "gone" as in deceased. She was surprised Theo hadn't mentioned that.

"I'm sorry about your parents."

"It's been a while, but thank you. They died in a car accident on the mainland."

They died together.

She closed her eyes for a second, trying to suppress a wave of grief. At least one of them hadn't left the other wondering where they'd gone wrong. Or if they could have done something—*anything*—differently.

Not a healthy avenue to pursue.

With as much PTSD as she'd treated, you'd think she'd be able to recognize it in herself. The problem was, she *did* recognize it. There just wasn't anything she could do about it. Things were the way they were, and no railing against fate was going to change it.

Mark was dead. His life cut short in a single defining moment.

Six months before they were supposed to be married.

"It's hard losing someone you care about."

The words came out of their own volition, making her frown. She needed to change the subject before it brought back even more memories. Ones that were better off left behind her.

"So, your aunt is a good cook?"

He pushed away from the counter, his tenseness evaporating. "One of the best on the island. Besides managing this place, she caters special events here on the island."

"Wow. I think I remember Theo saying something about the caterer being related to you. Is that your aunt?"

"If he called her Cecilia Patera, then, yes. She's really the only woman on the island who cooks for a living. Her moussaka is out of this world. They even serve some of her *meze* at Stavros's *taverna*. You've been there?"

"Only once. The owner was a little gruff."

Deakin's head tilted. "Really? That doesn't sound like Stavros. But I guess everyone can have an off day."

The man hadn't been mean, he'd just answered someone a little more curtly than she'd liked and that had been enough for her. She hadn't been back since.

"I'm sure that's what it was. Anyway, since I have destroyed my sense of hearing as well as your frying pan, I think I'll take you up on your offer of moussaka, if it's really okay. I can just bring a portion home and eat it here, though. I don't want to inconvenience you."

"I wouldn't have offered if it was an inconvenience. Or I could make you a quick omelet if you have your heart set on eggs."

"I actually love moussaka, so no. Eggs just seemed quick and easy."

The right side of his mouth went up. It was then she realized that she couldn't see his burns at all. Because that side of his face was angled away from her. But even if that crooked smile *was* a result of whatever had happened to him, it didn't make it any less sexy.

"Not so quick and not so easy, from the looks of it."

"Only because I was distracted," she protested with a smile.

He glanced toward the television, which was off. "Oh? By what?"

By thoughts of orange juice and…and her mysterious neighbor. But she was not going to say that out loud. He would kick her out if he suspected she was daydreaming about him.

She wasn't. She was just…thinking about life and the strange ways that paths intersected. And sometimes came to a dead end.

She shifted as a familiar heaviness in her chest made itself known.

There was nothing you could have done, Lea.

The voice inside her head came back with

its customary rejoinder: *How do you know that for sure?*

She couldn't know. She would never know. And even if she became convinced she'd missed a whole barrage of symptoms—which she hadn't—it was too late now.

Deakin was still waiting for her response.

She glanced out the window over the sink and caught sight of the gorgeous sunset. "By that." She motioned toward the sight, mentally crossing her fingers.

He put his elbows on the counter to get low enough to look out the window. "It is beautiful. I have the same view from the kitchen in the main house."

He might think it was a pretty view, but it didn't go deeper than an objective observation. How did she know that? There had been no emotion in the statement. No softening of his eyes. No smile the way he had when she'd changed the subject a few minutes ago.

"It's pretty breathtaking." She tried again to prod him lightly, not even sure what she was looking for.

"Yes, it is. Are you ready?" He had already turned away from the window, was coming around to the other side of the counter and checking the knobs on the stove.

"I already turned them off."

"Sometimes they stick."

No, they didn't. She'd heard the click as they snapped off.

Rather than be offended by his double-checking, she felt a rush of sympathy go through her. More and more she was convinced that something bad had happened to him very close to home. And those scars were old, so it had been a while ago. Long enough for him to have stopped needing to check knobs on a stove. Or was it...?

Leaving the cottage, he indicated the way down a cobblestone pathway that led to the main house. The harsh heat of the day was giving way to cooler temperatures now that the sun was going down. Even so, she was very glad the cottage was air-conditioned.

"Have you been in the house itself yet?" he asked.

"No, but it's beautiful from the outside."

"Yes, my parents did a nice job on it when it was built."

Her eyes skipped to the white boathouse near the shore. "You're very lucky to live so close to the water. It's a shame you aren't here very often to enjoy it. I would be in that boat every chance I got."

His steps faltered for a second, before he

continued on. "I go out in it every time I'm home."

"I bet it's gorgeous out there on the water."

"I guess it is." He glanced back at her. "I'll probably go out at least once while I'm here. You're welcome to join me if you'd like."

"Oh, I wasn't angling for an invitation. I'm sorry if it came across that way."

"It didn't."

Lea wasn't sure how she felt about going out on the water with him. There was something about him that made her uneasy.

She decided to sidestep the subject without making it too obvious. "Did you grow up in this house?"

"Yes."

She waited for him to elaborate, or tell her how long he'd lived there, but he didn't. By the time she tried to think of something else to break what was becoming an uncomfortable silence they were at the front door. Dark and heavy, it loomed over the small porch.

Or maybe it was her thoughts that were dark.

The main house hadn't seemed ominous before.

He opened it, motioning her through the entryway, and the feeling instantly went away. White tile flooring blended into equally white walls. It might have come across as spartan and cold except for the touches here and there of an azure blue that reminded Lea of the warm ocean waters that surrounded the island. It was there in a painting. In the pillows she could see through the arched doorway of the living room. It had been professionally decorated.

"I didn't expect the inside to look like this."

She couldn't stop the words. She thought the cottage was lovely and homey, but this was head and shoulders above the quaintness of where she was staying. It was ultra-formal and elegant. And somehow it didn't match Deakin at all.

He should be surrounded by brown furnishings and dark shadowy corners.

No, he shouldn't. That would be depressing.

Except it wouldn't. It would match what she sensed was inside him: hidden recesses that he revealed to no one.

She tensed. Hadn't she come across that before? Looking back, she wasn't sure how she could have missed those signs in Mark. Only she'd been young and in love, and Mark had had a way of flashing that carefree smile of his in a way that had seemed so genuine.

Wasn't that how emotional scars in people were overlooked until it was too late?

As if on cue, Deakin turned back, his scars appearing in stark contrast as the light from the doorway poured over them. "How did you expect it to look?"

"Don't get me wrong…it's extremely elegant." There was no way she could give voice to her thoughts from a moment earlier. *No way. No how.* "It's just very different from the cottage."

"My aunt had a hand in decorating the cottage. It's where I normally live when I come here. The house is rented out most of the year. The people who were going to rent it this month backed out because of the earthquake."

"Your aunt didn't help decorate the main house."

It was a statement. Not a question. There was no way the same person had had a hand in *this* house, although a skilled interior decorator could probably pull off two such divergent spaces.

"No." He swept a hand around the foyer. "This was all my parents' doing."

He said it as if it was not the way *he* would have done things.

"Are you going to redo it?"

"No."

The single word answer didn't invite discussion. Instead she studied the textured paint on the walls and the pricey rugs on the floor and changed the topic to something a little more neutral.

"Your guests must love staying here."

His eyes closed for a split second. In gratitude? She had no idea.

He tossed a set of keys and the remote he'd had at the cottage onto a nearby console table. "They seem to like it."

"Is there another remote for the alarm at the cottage?" She allowed a glimmer of a smile to play across her face. "In case I decide to cook again at some point?" The scent of something warm and inviting curled around her nostrils. "Although if that heavenly aroma is what I think it is I may have to hire your aunt to cook all my meals for me."

"I'm sure she would be happy to."

Lea had a feeling *he* might be happy if she did that as well.

"Seriously, do you want the cottage stove to be off-limits? Just say the word. I don't want you to worry about me setting the place on fire every time I'm in the kitchen."

"I'm not."

He wasn't what? Worried? Because the stiff set of his posture as he walked in the direction of the living room said something different.

"I'll give you a quick tour while dinner finishes heating."

They went through the archway, and her eyes tracked from thing to thing.

"This space is pretty obvious…"

The blue pillows she'd noticed earlier were set in precise rows along the back of the couch. It reminded her of suture lines. She did her best to hide the shiver that went through her. It was only her imagination. Or maybe just a reaction to the whole smoke alarm encounter.

She almost hadn't noticed that he'd shaved the stubble off his face sometime this evening. His hair was still on the longish side, but it was thick and glossy now, and her fingers suddenly itched to touch one of the dark wavy locks as he came to a stop. The man looked like a Greek god out of a legend.

She dragged her gaze back to the room when he turned to face her, and tried to shut the door on the shot of pure hormones that jetted through her.

Dust. Look for dust. A cobweb. Anything!

The perfectly square coffee table in front of her held a stack of magazines about boats, a white plaster lighthouse and a tray that held three blue candles. Not a speck of dust.

"Does your aunt clean the place after guests leave?"

"No, I hire a service to come in once a week.

My aunt must have asked them to come in for my arrival."

So he'd known exactly when he was coming home? Why had no one warned her before he arrived? "Does Theo know you're here?"

"Not yet. I didn't give him my exact itinerary. I figured I'd stop in at the clinic and then come straight home if it wasn't overrun with patients. I hoped to catch him there, but obviously not if he's taking a personal day. I'll call him in the morning."

"Patients seem to come in spurts. Some days we can hardly keep up. Other days we're twiddling our thumbs—like this afternoon."

"How are you getting to and from the clinic?"

She shifted her weight to the other foot. "Well, there's a…um…a bicycle stored behind the cottage. I hope you don't mind I've been borrowing it?"

"Why don't you take the car? It's there for guests—surely Cecilia told you about it?"

"She did, but I was worried about aftershocks right after I vacated my hotel. I figured I could navigate a bicycle off the road in case of a car accident or a traffic jam. And then, once that danger had passed, I'd just got used to riding in. It helps me enjoy the beauty of the island."

"It's not quite as beautiful as it once was."

"You should have seen it right after the quake hit. It was awful."

The memory of the ground shuddering beneath her feet, of plaster cracking and sheeting off the walls in her hotel room, stopped any lingering feeling of attraction in its tracks. She'd crawled under the bed, hoping the roof wasn't going to cave in on top of her. It had seemed like forever before the ground tremors had subsided, when in reality it had probably only lasted a few minutes.

"I'm sorry you had to go through that."

Her brows went up. "I'm sorry *anyone* had to go through it. It was terrible."

"I'm sure it was." He dragged a hand through his hair. "There was no way I could have come any sooner—my contract was unbreakable. I saw the reports on the news when I was sitting in a bar in Africa. Theo called as I was watching, and once I got off the phone with him I called everyone I could think of to see if they were okay."

They walked through the door to the dining room—another opulent space, where a huge glass-topped table crouched beneath a low chandelier. The surface, like the coffee table in the living room, was devoid of dust or even a single smudged fingerprint.

It bothered her, somehow. This didn't look

like a place where a family might recount the minutiae of their day. Or where a child might spill a glass of milk and not live in fear of messing up something. Instead it reeked of formal place settings and expensive crystal. A place where business negotiations were hammered out.

Had Deakin eaten here as a child? God, she hoped not. She could just picture him eating a bowl of breakfast cereal all by himself. But maybe it hadn't been that way at all. Maybe he was from a big family who laughed their way through life.

"Do you have more family on the island?"

"You mean siblings?" He shook his head. "Nope. I'm an only child."

So no under the table kicking of a little sister or brother. No food fights or handing nontasty morsels to the family dog. There was no sign that a pet of any kind had ever lived in this house.

Lea's childhood home had been messy and chaotic, with dogs and rabbits and horse shows through the local club. But she wouldn't trade it for the world. Medical school had been too grueling for her to have pets, but she certainly planned on having one or two once she got settled. In fact she and Mark had visited a shelter one time, just a week before he died.

Thank goodness they hadn't adopted a pet that day.

A fresh bout of anger went through her, even though he'd been gone more than a year. Ten years from now she would probably feel just as bewildered, could understand the grief and anger of other loved ones who'd been left behind just as suddenly.

"I'm an only child as well."

She wasn't going to delve beyond that, because she didn't know enough about him to trade childhood snapshots. Not yet, anyway. And probably not ever, since she wouldn't see him again once she'd left the island.

A pang went through her at the thought of going back to Toronto. As much as she loved her parents and her adopted city, she had put down the first tiny threads of roots on Mythelios. The second she'd stepped onto the island there'd been a sense of home. Of belonging. Maybe because of her Greek heritage. But her savings would eventually run out and she would have to go back to work.

The question was where.

He stopped in the doorway of the kitchen and turned toward her, propping his left shoulder against the door frame and crossing his arms. "It must have been quite an adjustment moving to Canada, then."

She had to backtrack for a second to realize he was talking about her being an only child.

"In some ways. But I think it made it easier for me to adapt. Toronto has a lot of immigrants, but I went to school. I had to learn English quickly in order to survive. Sink or swim. I swam."

And Mark hadn't.

He pursed his lips. "You've left your position there, though. Where are you off to next? Back to Canada?"

It was as if he'd read her mind. "I'm not sure yet. I haven't thought that far ahead."

Her parents were there. And yet the last thing she wanted to do was face her and Mark's old apartment. She'd have to, though, even if just to pack up her things. *His* belongings were long gone. Mark's mom and dad had been tasked with the heartbreaking job of sorting through everything and deciding what to do with his personal items. She'd spent the week in a hotel to give them some privacy. That had been many months ago, but the sharp sting of those days still remained.

"I understand how that is."

His arms dropped to his sides, his posture opening up as if he really did understand her uncertainty.

Glancing over his shoulder, he said, "I think

dinner is probably just about ready. Are you okay with eating out on the back deck? It should be cooling off outside by now."

"Outside sounds wonderful." She hoped her tone didn't give away how relieved she was they were not to be seated at opposite ends of that enormous table.

The right side of his mouth kicked up in a way that said he was just as glad. "Good. Then if you'll get the plates out of that cabinet by the sink, I'll get the pan out of the oven."

Opening the glass-fronted cabinet, she pulled down two ornate pieces of china, giving a quick wrinkle of her nose that she hoped he wouldn't see. Maybe their conversation would be a little less brittle than the dinnerware. Maybe they could even put that awkward first meeting behind them and get off on a better foot. For as long as they both were here.

She grimaced at how close that was to another sentence. If Mark had lived they would be married. But he hadn't. And they weren't. And Lea had no plans to leap into another romance anytime soon.

Right now she just needed to focus on putting that painful period in her life behind her. While she never would have wished Mythelios's earthquake on anyone, it had served to take her mind off herself and focus on doing good for those on the island. Didn't she always tell her patients that giving back to others was a great way to derail self-pity? She should have taken a page from her own book months ago. But she hadn't been ready to let go of the apartment which was a last connection to her fiancé.

She took a deep breath and accepted the steaming plate Deakin handed her with a murmured thank-you.

One thing was for sure, though. She was never getting involved with another man who carried a truckload of baggage. If she dated again, she was picking someone fun. Someone full of sunshine and light.

No brooding. No past trauma.

She gave a mental pinky-swear…to herself.

Happy, cheerful, and an eternal optimist. That was the best prescription she could think of.

And what better place to start than with herself?

CHAPTER THREE

"WHY DIDN'T YOU tell me you were arriving yesterday, Deak? Cailey and I would have picked you up. Did you fly in or take the ferry?"

Theo stood in the doorway to the exam room his patient had just exited, his frowning countenance not fooling anyone. His friend was glad to see him.

"I flew. It was a pretty bumpy landing. I guess they'll resurface the runway eventually. My aunt said it got damaged pretty badly."

"It was cracked in half. They did what they could to get it up and running again." He grinned. "I'm glad you could finally join the party."

Setting his laptop on the counter top, he walked over and gave Theo a quick brotherly slap on the back. "From what I've heard you're doing quite a bit of partying. I didn't want to disturb your love-nest."

Theo was one of the few people he'd never

felt judged by. As kids he, Chris and Eri had never ogled his scars, but they hadn't tiptoed around them either. They'd accepted them, just like they'd accepted him—something his parents had never seemed able to do after the fire.

He'd never told them the whole truth. It wouldn't have helped the situation and it would have just made life harder for Ville, whose home life had been a million times worse than his. At least Deakin's parents hadn't *hit* him. They'd just frozen him out emotionally instead.

"Love-nest? Really?" He paused. "Cailey's pregnant. I wasn't sure if you'd heard."

Deakin's brows went up and he slapped his friend's back again. Hard enough to make Theo grunt this time. "No, you conveniently omitted that fact during our first phone conversation."

"Well, since it happened sometime *after* that call…" He chuckled. "Oh, you've met Lea Risi, haven't you?"

Deakin picked up his laptop, setting it on the table near the door. "She's living almost under my roof, so it's kind of hard to miss her. Another thing you cleverly omitted to mention."

"We can move her somewhere else if having her there bothers you. Cecilia kind of insisted when the hotel was evacuated. I could always check with Cailey and move her into our house."

"No. I'll survive. It's not like I'll be here for a year or anything."

"You never know."

His chest tightened. "Oh, I *know*."

Better change the subject before they got into it. He and Theo had already gone round and round enough times on this particular subject.

"So, what about this whole fundraising bachelor auction thing Cecelia has told me about? *I* don't have to do anything for it, right?"

"Well, since I'm out of the running, being an expectant father and all…"

Deakin made a sound that was half-grunt, half-laugh. "You must have wanted out of that auction really bad."

"Um…no. That's not quite how things worked. I never expected to meet someone and… Well, anyway, now that you're here you can take my place in the auction. The earthquake decimated our funds. And our CT scanner is on the fritz. It has to be repaired or replaced."

"Not interested. I already did that freak show of a calendar. Besides, I wouldn't bring in enough for a photocopier, much less a CT machine."

The thought of standing on some stage having people bid—or not bid—on his "worth" gave him the heebie-jeebies. Or, worse, having some little old lady place a pity bid on him that had him scrubbing her kitchen sink or something.

"I'd also appreciate it if you'd ask Petra to take down that calendar hanging in the reception area. At least for the month of July."

"Ha! That would be a negative, since that calendar has already brought in several thousand euros. If you want it down, *you* ask her."

And risk getting on Petra's wrong side? Although it might be worth it this time. Deakin's picture on the calendar was for the month of July, which was just over a week away. He didn't want *anyone* seeing that snapshot, especially not Lea.

He wasn't sure why that thought bothered him more than having other people see it. Maybe because he'd grown up on this island and they all knew him—knew his history. She didn't, and he didn't want her asking anyone about the incident which had seared a roadmap of scars into the left side of his chest.

There were areas of it that had never regained sensation, the nerves permanently damaged. He would never again feel the scrape of a woman's fingertips on those parts of his body.

His throat tightened. Not that he routinely invited women into his bedroom, for the very same reason that he didn't want that calendar out there for the world to see.

Lea would probably think he'd been on some kind of ego trip during that whole photo shoot. That was the furthest thing from the truth. He hadn't wanted to do it, but their trust fund money from Mopaxeni Shipping had been running short for the year. So they had concocted the stupid scheme to get some local guys on a calendar, figuring some of the islanders might be keen to help fund the clinic.

One of the subjects had had a gall stone attack the day of the photo shoot, so Deakin had been an emergency substitute to save the day—such as it was. He hadn't even looked at the actual shot when it had been sent over— had just checked the "accept" box and sent the envelope back to the photographer.

The thought of Lea seeing how far down his scars went made him queasy. He'd caught her studying his neck when she thought he wasn't looking. Several times, in fact. He'd even almost balked about getting his hair cut this morning, because the longer it was, the more it covered. But that would have been admitting that Lea's curious glances disturbed him on some level. So he'd gone to his aunt and asked her to do the deed. She had, and four inches of shaggy growth had ended up on her kitchen floor.

He hadn't seen Lea since it had been cut. Would her glance skate over him like it had before? It didn't matter. His scars were a reality he dealt with every single day. No amount of hair was going to change that. He was damned lucky his arm and his hand had been spared. He'd turned to the side just in time.

Ville had been even more fortunate. He'd been standing on the far side of him during the explosion and his burns had reached second degree, missing third by a narrow margin.

"Well, the calendar was my first and last hurrah. No auction for me. No one would bid on me anyway."

Theo sighed. "Give yourself a little credit, Deak. There are plenty of women who would *love* to have a chance to place that winning bid."

"No way. Besides, I'm not staying on Mythelios long enough for anyone to put in a claim."

His friend laughed. "It's a bachelor auction. Not a mail order husband scheme."

That made Deakin grin. He'd forgotten how much he enjoyed these exchanges with his friends. "Well, I'm sure there are plenty of other guys who would jump at the chance to be raffled off."

"Auctioned," Theo corrected.

"Same thing."

Theo snapped his fingers. "I just remembered. I called in to the clinic at Naxos to order supplies. Any chance you could do a boat-run over there and pick it up in the next couple of days? Sending it by courier will just up the cost, and we're trying to pare down expenses as much as possible."

"Sure—not a problem."

"Take Lea with you, if you can. She's been on this island since the earthquake and she could probably use a little time away."

Great. He wished Theo had relayed that little tidbit *before* he'd agreed to go. "She's welcome to come if she wants to. But if she doesn't…" He forced a shrug that he hoped showed indifference.

A woman he recognized appeared in the doorway. Cailey Tomaras. Always a beautiful woman, she practically glowed now. Pregnancy hormones? Or was this what love did to you?

It took one touch of her hand on Theo's arm to answer that question. His face was totally transformed, with a smile crinkling the corners of his eyes. Deakin couldn't help but stare. His friend was *happy*. Truly happy.

Hell. What was that even like? He wasn't sure he knew anymore. Traveling from one outpost to another left little time to dissect his feelings. Or anything else.

Which was what he'd wanted when he'd left his parents' home, leaving it as a mausoleum— a reminder of all the reasons he'd moved away from the island.

His aunt had been bugging him to revamp the place for ages. When her requests had begun to show concern he'd let her do the cottage. He'd gotten into the habit of staying there. Until it had been occupied by a certain beautiful psychiatrist, forcing him back into the main house.

And he hated it there just as much today as he had when he'd lived in it as a teenager. Maybe it was time to let Aunt Cecilia have her way with it.

Theo turned toward him, forcing him from his thoughts. "Deak, you remember Cailey?"

"Yes, of course. Good to see you again."

"You as well." She shook his hand. "It's been a while. Theo talks about you a lot."

He tensed for a moment before he realized she probably wasn't referring to his past. There was no condemnation in her eyes, nor any hint of unease. Her eyes had skipped over his scars, but they hadn't lingered the way Lea's had.

Smiling, he tipped his head toward Theo. "All bad, if I know this guy."

"Actually, it was all good. Theo thinks a lot of you, Ares and Chris."

Cailey's fingers reached for Theo's, linking them together. Another shaft of unease went through Deakin's gut and then was gone.

She looked up at Theo. "Are we still on for lunch?"

"Of course. How are you feeling?"

"Better. Hungry." She glanced at Deakin. "You've heard our news?"

"Yes, congratulations."

"Thank you. We're pretty excited. Do you want to join us for lunch?"

And have their happiness remind him of all the things he would never have? Not likely. He knew that was unfair to Theo, and he was genuinely happy for his friend, but it was a shock to have the first one of their group travel down *this* particular path. He certainly hadn't seen it coming.

"Thank you, but I think Lea is entering the sign-in sheets into the patient records and she wants to ask me about some of them." It was only a half-lie.

Theo nodded. "I asked her to take that over for a while."

A while? That sounded a little too open-ended for his peace of mind.

"How long is she going to be here?" he asked, aiming for casual interest but not entirely sure he'd nailed it.

Theo shrugged. "I haven't thought that far in advance."

Weren't those almost the exact words Lea had used when he'd asked about her plans?

"Maybe she'll stay. She seems to really like it here." Cailey smiled.

The pain in his gut was back. "I doubt it. She was at a huge hospital in Toronto. I'm sure she's got better places to choose than Mythelios."

"You never know. Stranger things have happened." Theo's fingers squeezed his wife's. "Hey, when you get a chance can you go by the *taverna* and have a drink for me?"

"You normally have to drink yourself in order for it to do any good."

"I'm serious. Stavros hasn't been feeling well recently, but whenever anyone tries to talk to him about it he basically tells them to go to hell."

Stavros's *taverna* was a local legend, visited by islanders and tourists alike.

"Not feeling well is a pretty vague description."

Theo let go of Cailey's hand and wrapped his arm around her waist instead. "He's been having headaches. And I've been hearing over the last week or so that he's also been really grumpy."

"Lea mentioned that he'd rubbed her up the wrong way. She didn't use those exact words, but it was the idea I got."

"That's definitely not like him." Cailey leaned her head on Theo's arm.

These two had it bad. But he guessed since they were having a child together that was probably a *good* thing.

"Okay, I'll check on him. And I'll get those supplies. Does it have to be today?"

"There's nothing we need right this minute, no. Just whenever you get to it. Stavros, on the other hand, worries me. If you can't go I'll make time."

"I'll do it. I kind of like the old man."

"Thanks. And on that note, we're off. Call if you need us. And don't try to take over Lea's job."

"I have no plans for doing that."

He wasn't really meeting Lea to discuss the patient records anyway. He'd made that up to get out of going to lunch. Maybe he'd head over to Stavros' place and get a feel for whatever it was Theo was worried about.

At noon?

Probably not the best idea. The *taverna* would be packed. He'd have to wait until normal business hours.

Well, he would just go out and see if he could scrounge up a patient to treat, then. Anything to get his mind off the thought that Cailey really might ask Lea to stay at the clinic. For good.

Why do you even care, Deakin?

He shouldn't. There was no reason to. *He* wasn't staying on the island, so it shouldn't matter at all to him.

All he knew was that it did. And he had no idea why.

The Serenity Gardens had become almost as much of a haven to her as it was to her patients. This was one of the few places that had been left untouched by the earthquake. It was a calm oasis, with the gentle waves lapping in the background becoming white noise that soothed the senses while helping mute the voices that weren't right next to you. It provided an additional sense of privacy.

Some parts of the gardens were open to the public, with curving sidewalks and shady places where people could gather and quietly converse. There were signs that asked for cell phones to be silenced and conversations kept low and discreet. The place where Lea and her current patient were meeting had a thick braided rope stretched between two trellises to keep visitors from inadvertently wandering in and interrupting her sessions.

Those two trellises, woven through with flowering vines, created a natural screen for her makeshift office. It was as private as any of the exam rooms inside the clinic. But it sure was a whole lot more attractive. She'd already noticed a difference, compared with the tiny supply closet she'd used when she'd first arrived. The natural setting created intimacy and calmed frayed nerves. Including her own.

"I just don't get why my neighbor's house was totally destroyed and mine wasn't touched. It doesn't seem right."

She'd had several of this kind of patient. People who didn't understand the randomness of being spared while someone else had suffered terrible losses. She knew that pain first-hand.

"I don't have an answer. But you've reached out and provided a place for them to stay while they rebuild."

"They should probably be the ones here talking to you, not me. And that makes me feel even more selfish. They seem to be coping so much better than I am."

"You don't know that for certain. People can hide a lot."

As she'd found out the hard way. And she'd bet the handsome plastic surgeon she'd met three days ago had plenty to hide, too.

Why was she even *thinking* about him? She'd only seen him in passing over the last day or so. He'd been as gruff during those encounters as he'd been during their first meeting, making her sigh in defeat. And he'd made no more surprise visits to the cottage.

Of course she'd been pretty careful about keeping an eye on the stove since then. No more burned eggs. No more smoke alarms. And no more Deakin.

She wasn't sure how she felt about that.

Cailey had made kind of a strange comment yesterday. She'd asked how Lea was enjoying working at the clinic, and then shocked her by saying that she'd made quite an impact on the island in the short time she'd been there.

She didn't know about that, but the island had certainly made an impact on *her*.

If she could find a place like this for her next position she would be in heaven. She had a feeling there weren't many islands like Mythelios in the world, though. So she'd better enjoy every second she was there. Because it would eventually come to an end.

And she was beginning to hate that thought.

She turned her attention back to her patient. "It sounds like you're doing all the right things. You're helping your neighbor weather this storm, and I promise you they will remember this. You've eased the way for them. Best of all, you're providing aid you might not have been able to had your own house been damaged or destroyed."

"I know, but…"

"It still hurts?"

A muscle pulsed in the man's cheek as he fought to get control of whatever was going on inside him. Finally, he said, "Yes. It does."

"And that's okay. As long as you don't let it take control of your life."

"That's why I'm here. Just talking about it helps, and knowing someone else understands. I didn't want to worry my wife by breaking down in front of her."

She did understand—even if she didn't agree with him hiding all this from his wife. And her words about not letting guilt take control of his life had come out of the bitter reality of her own recent past.

"You are not the only one going through this. So take heart."

He took a deep breath and then blew it out, climbing to his feet. "Thank you. I don't think the clinic has ever had a psychiatrist before. Or if it did I never knew about it."

She didn't think it had. There were a couple of psychologists on the island, with private practices, but she'd already had a couple of referrals from them. This patient being one of them. They were overrun with people needing assistance for mental health issues, and since Lea was able to prescribe medication, whereas they weren't, she had gradually shifted from just seeing whatever patient came through the doors of the clinic, to seeing people within her own specialty.

She imagined Deakin and some of the others were now taking up some of the slack in other areas.

"I'm just glad the clinic has allowed me to help where I can."

"I certainly appreciate it." He reached out to shake her hand. "Thanks again. Can I call you if I need you? Or if my wife or neighbors need you?"

"Of course. You have my card. Go home. Talk to your wife. Tell her just what you told me. I bet she'll understand more than you know."

"I'll try."

That was all any of them could do.

"Good."

She walked him out and unhooked the rope to let him pass by. This was her last scheduled patient of the day. The man disappeared around the corner and Lea turned back to write up her notes and put them in his file.

Would he be back? Maybe. If he was still having trouble coping, then she hoped he would.

Head down in her notes, she jumped when someone said her name.

She looked up to find Deakin standing over her chair. And had to do a double-take. Something was different about him. She tilted her head and studied his face, her gaze trailing up the right side of his jaw to where his hair created a shadow. *Wait.* There *was* no shadow.

His hair was gone.

Well, not gone. But it was certainly shorter than it had been.

Her insides dipped. And she hadn't even managed to touch it…

Her face burned with white heat. How had *that* thought gotten in there? And how had she missed the distinctive click as the rope barrier was unhooked? A little warning might have been good. God, was her face as red as it felt?

"I'm glad I wasn't in here with a patient."

That had come out a little gruffer than she'd intended it to, because his appearance—his *changed* appearance—had startled her so much.

She had to admit his haircut suited him. Cut to just above his collar, it retained a tiny curl at the bottom that hinted of the waves he'd had chopped off. The rest was crisp and clean and…

She still wanted to run her fingers through it.

Dammit!

"I checked with Petra. She said your patient left a few minutes ago. Am I disturbing you?"

Yes. But not in the way he meant. If his scruffy appearance at the clinic three days ago had knocked her for a loop, this new Deakin— handsome, sophisticated Deakin—was knocking her into the stratosphere.

To keep him from standing there, she motioned him to the seat across from hers. Maybe if he was sitting she wouldn't have as much to stare at.

Nope. He dropped into the chair and propped an ankle on his other knee. He was now at her eye level. A dangerous place for both of them.

"What can I do for you?"

He uncrossed his legs, leaned forward and rested his elbows on his knees. "I think I might be in need of your services."

Shock rolled through her. "Excuse me?"

There was no way she was taking Deakin on as a patient unless it was a life or death situation. Not with the way her system had heated up just at the sight of him.

"Since we're colleagues at the same clinic, it might be better if I referred you to—"

His elbows came off his knees in a hurry and he went stock still. "Hell, it's not for *me*. What made you think that?"

"Well, you just said you thought you might be in need…" She blinked. "I don't understand."

And she really didn't.

"I guess I didn't phrase that very well."

The tight set of his lips made her wonder if he was going to get up and leave. But he didn't.

After a few seconds, he went on. "You said when you went to Stavros's *taverna* that he was… What was the word you used?"

Trying to remember a specific word right now was going to be great fun. She cast around in her head, trying to dredge up that conversation.

"I think I said he was gruff."

He'd reminded her of a grumpy old man, even though he wasn't all that elderly. He'd mentioned something about a headache and had downed a couple of pills, but his attitude had persisted, ending with him snapping at someone.

"Yeah. *Gruff.* Theo mentioned that as well. And he's worried about him."

"I'm sure everyone is on edge after the quake. And he has a lot of people coming through the bar. It was packed the day I was there."

He nodded. "Maybe it's just that. But since I was planning on taking some downtime tonight and going over there anyway, I thought maybe you could go with me."

Her teeth caught her lower lip to keep her jaw from dropping. Was he asking her *out*?

As if he knew the direction her thoughts were headed, he narrowed his eyes. "I thought you could give me your…erm…*professional* opinion while we're there. If you don't have plans, that is."

Maybe it was the fact that she'd already misunderstood his motive for asking her to go that made her bristle slightly at the way he'd said it. "'Professional' opinion. You mean you want me to read his palm? Peer at his tea leaves?"

"Of course not."

His hand went to the side of his jaw before scrubbing over the scars on his neck. She doubted he was even aware he was doing it.

"I just want someone there who can get a read on whether he's struggling with the after effects of the earthquake or if there's something else going on. Some physiological cause."

"Sometimes it's both."

"Which is why I'd like you to be there when I talk to him. Please."

The word tacked onto the end told her Deakin really was worried. Or maybe it was Theo's concern that was coming through.

Evidently the Stavros she had met that night in the bar wasn't the same man the community was used to seeing. Which meant she was going to go. Because there was no way she could ignore a plea like Deakin's. She had a feeling asking for her opinion hadn't come easily for this plastic surgeon.

"Okay. I'll tell you what I think—but if the man doesn't want help nothing in this world is going to convince him to accept it."

"I'm not going to suggest anything." He paused. "He's a friend. I want to make sure he's okay."

"And if he's not?"

"Then I'm going to drag Theo, Cailey and whoever else I can find down to that bar and make Stavros listen. We might not be able to force him to admit something's wrong, but we sure as hell can force him to hear us out."

A wave of admiration swept over her. "That *taverna* owner is a lucky man. Not everyone has friends like you and Theo."

Mark had always been a bit of a loner. That was one of the things that had attracted her to him initially. After the frenetic pace of medical school it had been nice to come home to a quiet house. Looking back, she knew warning bells should have been going off even then. But he'd seemed uncomplicated and easy going. He'd never fought. Had rarely gone against her in anything. And he'd been a loyal and faithful companion.

Until he hadn't.

He hadn't seemed depressed. He'd smiled, laughed at her jokes and had seemed to enjoy life.

But it had all been an act. Or had she only seen what she'd wanted to see? Made him into something she needed him to be?

Guilt sloshed over her once again in a wave that robbed her of oxygen. She struggled to break free of its grip and gulped down a huge breath.

"Stavros is a fixture on this island. I think there are a whole lot of people who would stand beside him. It's just that, from what I've seen, people are so busy trying to make insurance claims and do repairs on their homes that noticing little changes in someone's personality is brushed aside."

Another sliver pierced her heart.

Had she done that with Mark? Brushed aside the little changes that might have signaled her to take action? She would never know. Not now.

Maybe Stavros was no different from any of the other earthquake victims, but something was telling Deakin not to laugh it off as the workings of a grump. So neither would she. Not this time.

"So, are the rest of the clinic's patients covered for the day?" she asked.

"Yes, there are other doctors working the late shift, and they're all here."

"Great." She stuffed her laptop into her large shoulder bag. "I'll take the bike and then leave straight from the *taverna* to go home once we're done. Do you want to meet me there?"

"I think it'll look more natural to Stavros if we arrive together."

"Why?"

"Let's just say that I know how the man's mind works. If a woman suddenly joins me at the bar he's going to know immediately that something's up."

"Maybe he'll think I'm trying to wrangle an invitation to join you?"

"Not hardly!"

Before she could mull over those words, he turned and started walking, throwing over his shoulder, "I'll meet you in the parking area. I'm in the red Jeep."

She knew what he'd be driving, since they had offered to let her use the vehicle when she'd moved to the cottage. She'd refused.

But using someone else's bicycle doesn't bother you?

Three minutes later they were cruising down the main strip that ran across the island, heading south toward the spot where most of the island's restaurants and hotels were. Stavros's place was within walking distance of the clinic, but by parking there they wouldn't have to backtrack once they'd left the bar.

Parking wasn't the easiest, and being in the car with Deakin made her realize how much easier it was just to prop her bike up beside whatever store she was going to and forget about it. As it was, it took longer to find a spot than it had to drive to the bar. But they finally located one that had just been vacated and Deakin turned off the ignition.

"Do you have a drink of choice?"

"Um… I didn't realize I was going to be drinking."

Up went his brows. "Stavros is a smart man. We want to try and catch him off guard so he talks to us."

It went against her better judgment, but she finally said, "A strawberry daiquiri, then."

"I would have guessed rum and Coke. Or Scotch on the rocks."

Why was that? Did he not think she could be a frou-frou girl when she wanted to be? Something about that stung.

Her main reason for getting a fruity drink was so that she could take her time sipping it without looking like an oddball. Especially since she didn't drink all that much. The only time she'd gone to Stavros's had been when she'd had to vacate her hotel room. The bar had been the closest place to get something to eat.

She decided to come back with a quip. "It all depends on my mood."

"Ah. I'll have to remember that." A flicker of dark humor seemed to light up those brown eyes. "And what would your mood be tonight?"

Warmth bloomed in her belly.

He's not…flirting with me. Is he?

She decided to test the waters, even though an alarm louder than his smoke detector was currently going off in her head. "My mood? Contemplative."

It wasn't a lie. She was doing her best to figure this out as she went along. So far she was failing on every count.

"A daiquiri is contemplative?"

"It can be anything I choose it to be." She gave him a grin. Okay, he might not be flirting, but it was kind of fun to sit here throwing quips back and forth. "What are *you* drinking?"

His gaze dropped to her mouth and held for a brief moment. Then he shut his eyes tight. When he reopened them, he said, "Whiskey. I'm drinking whiskey."

His opened his door before she could come up with anything to say to that. She hurried to follow suit, embarrassed heat leaking into her face. Deakin clicked a button on his key fob to lock the vehicle. She tried to dredge up some professional conversation, even though she just wanted to grab his arm and ask him to go back in time to a few seconds ago, when the weight of the world had so briefly lifted from her shoulders.

"Anything more I should know about Stavros before I go in?"

"Just that he's owned the *taverna* for as long as I can remember, and he knows almost everyone who lives here. He's good to the tourists who visit and helps whoever needs it. He's a genuinely nice guy."

That hadn't been the impression *she'd* gotten, but she would take Deakin's word for it. Tragedy did strange things to people.

Like sending them running to another place.

That wasn't what she was doing. Was it?

"It's been a while since you've been here, right? Could he simply have changed?"

"Stavros has been the same for as long as I've known him—which is a long time. And Theo also mentioned something being off, and he *lives* on the island."

She reached for the door handle, pulling back when someone pushed through from the other side. A couple, their arms wrapped around each other, stumbled slightly as they came through, the woman giving a high-pitched squeal that raked down Lea's spine. The heavy door swung shut, with neither person offering to hold it for them. The pair was drunk. *Very* drunk.

Off they went across the street, weaving back and forth as they went. Lea watched them go, hoping against hope that they weren't going to get into a car.

They didn't—just kept staggering down the sidewalk, probably headed home.

Deakin frowned. "See? That wouldn't normally happen."

"What? Someone in a bar having too much to drink?"

"Believe it or not, no. Stavros usually keeps track, and he isn't afraid to cut people off when they're getting too close to their limit."

This time Lea was able to swing the door open without resistance. Deakin wrapped his fingers around the upper part of it and held it so she could go through.

She frowned almost immediately. The atmosphere was darker than she remembered, the lights dimmed almost as low as they would go. But she'd only been there once, so maybe it was her imagination.

Deakin paused as if taking stock of the place and then strode toward the bar, where the same white-haired man she remembered was pouring a drink. Even from where she stood she could see that the liquid had sloshed out of the glass a bit, causing Stavros to grab a towel and wipe up the spill.

He said something to the customer, who took the drink from him and walked to a nearby table.

It was loud. So loud she had trouble hearing the piped in music over the raucous sound of inebriation—which she hadn't realized had a specific sound until now.

Stavros's eyes came up and landed on Deakin. "Deak! Is that you? When the hell did you get home, and why did no one tell me?"

The man dropped his red towel onto the bar and came around to give him a hug. Lea moved closer, and Stavros spotted her.

"Did you bring a wife back with you?"

It wasn't strange that he didn't remember her, but to be mistaken for Deakin's *wife*…

Deakin chuckled, but it sounded forced. "No. No wife."

There was no *not yet* added to that phrase. It was as if he was never planning on getting married. Maybe he was a confirmed bachelor. Or maybe…

No, a woman would be a fool to let a few scars deter her from getting to know a man like this.

A man like *what*? He certainly wasn't the optimistic fun-loving guy she thought she was looking for.

She *wasn't* looking. Where had that come from?

Get a grip, Lea!

"No wife?" Stavros leaned an elbow on the bar's surface. "Are you crazy? They're fun. Had a few of them myself."

The syllables shot from his mouth in rapid staccato, accompanied by a wide grin.

Okay, this wasn't grumpy Stavros. This was manic Stavros. He had a feverish quality about him that made her look a little closer.

Deakin caught her eye and gave a slight nod. She wasn't sure if he'd read her mind and was agreeing with her, or if he wanted her to try to figure something out.

If it was the latter, there wasn't enough to go on yet. She gave a slight shrug.

"No wife," Deakin repeated. "This is a friend. Leanora Risi. She works with me at the clinic."

"Oh, yes. I thought you looked familiar. You had something to eat. No alcohol."

Deakin's brows shot up. "You don't drink?"

"I do on occasion."

Her face flamed for what seemed like the hundredth time that day. She wasn't going to discuss how much she did or didn't drink—especially since she'd already told Deakin she did.

"I'll have a strawberry daiquiri."

"Of course. And you, Deak? What'll you have?"

"How about a little more light? I've never seen it this dark in here."

"It keeps folks happy."

His words were still tumbling, end over end. And was that dilation of his pupils due to the low level of light? Or something else. Maybe the good bartender did more than just tend bar for the people of Mythelios.

She hooked an index finger and touched it to the inside of her left elbow, giving Deakin a slight raise of the eyebrows.

He shook his head—no. He didn't think Stavros was shooting up with anything.

"I'll have a whiskey, then."

A whiskey. He'd evidently been serious in the car when he'd said that was what he was drinking.

Stavros reclaimed his spot behind the bar and began mixing their drinks. In the middle of doing it he picked up a pill bottle and shook a couple of tablets into his hand. It wasn't a brown prescription bottle—it looked like something from over the counter.

"What are those?" she whispered to Deakin.

"I don't know. But Stavros has never taken anything before. At least not that I've ever seen."

The bartender stuck her drink in front of her. She picked it up and took a quick sip while he finished making Deakin's whiskey and handed it over.

"So, what have you been up to?" Stavros asked him.

"I've been in Africa for the last several months, working with an NGO."

"That's good…that's good. Now, if you'll excuse me…"

He moved away to take care of another customer.

"Is this how he was the last time you were here?" Deakin asked her.

She perched on the nearest barstool and took another sip of her drink. "No. Just the opposite. That evening he seemed sluggish and unhappy. He snapped at a man who had a problem with the way he'd mixed his drink."

Deakin set his glass down and stared across the bar at where Stavros was moving at warp speed. "Can you tell anything by watching him?"

"He's never had any personality changes like this before? No highs and lows?"

"He's always been just… *Stavros*. Unflappable. Unhurried. And that man knows his drinks. There is no way he would have mixed something incorrectly. Or gotten angry if someone had called him on it."

The next sip of her drink went down a little too smoothly. She swirled the contents of her glass. "Maybe you should come right out and ask him if he's feeling okay…see what he says."

Stavros opened a drawer behind the bar and looked for something, digging through the contents of the drawer, grizzled brows furrowed. He took a deep breath and pinched the bridge of his nose. As if giving up, he slammed the drawer shut and came around the bar, stopping in front of Deakin.

"How long are you home for?"

The tone was a little less friendly, this time.

"Not long. A month, maybe. Long enough to help with some of the clean-up."

The bartender's fingers repeated the squeeze against the upper part of his nose.

Deakin leaned closer, looking up into the man's face. "You feeling okay?"

Stavros's head whipped up and he stared at Deakin suspiciously. "What do you mean?"

"You seem a little flustered this evening. I thought you might be feeling under the weather."

Just like that, Stavros's demeanor changed from cheerful to angry. His hands, which had been lying on top of the bar, curled in on themselves, clenching into fists. "Maybe you should mind your own damn business, Deak."

"I'm just concerned about you. So is Theo."

"Well, don't be. I'm fine. Always have been.

Always will be. All you guys at the clinic should get off your high horses."

A red flag went up in her mind. It was the same attitude Mark had had any time she'd questioned one of his moods. He got defensive and tried to deflect attention away from himself. Only he had used avoidance, not confrontation.

"Hey, don't take it personally," Deakin said, holding up placating hands.

"You mean like your dad did all those years ago?"

Whoa. Lea had no idea what Stavros meant by that, but the effect the words had on Deakin was shocking. All the color leached from his face until it was the same shade as his pale scars. A pulse began throbbing in his temple. The bartender had definitely touched some kind of nerve.

Deflecting.

Just like Mark.

Deakin—and Theo—were right. Something was wrong with this man. He either didn't realize it or he was ignoring the problem, hoping it would go away.

But she'd learned the hard way that the problem—whatever it was—not only wouldn't go away, it would grow and grow and grow, until

Stavros…or maybe even Deakin…could no longer pretend that things were fine.

She just wasn't sure if that moment would be a month from now, a year from now, or if it was about to happen right before their eyes.

CHAPTER FOUR

DEAKIN'S FIRST INSTINCT was to put his fist into Stavros's mocking face. Theo's comment about no one remembering what had happened in the past was obviously not true. Stavros not only remembered, he'd just thrown it right in his face. Thank God he'd left Ville out of it.

Something warm pressed against his wrist, and when he looked down he saw it was Lea's hand. His own were curled into tight fists, just like his friend's had been a second or two ago.

Did Lea sense what he was feeling, or had she read his body language and decided to intervene?

Whatever it was, it acted like a wake-up call. He had no idea why Stavros would want to open that can of worms right here and now, but the man wasn't a fool. He'd had a reason, and Deakin thought he could guess what it was.

His friend gave him a mocking little salute and sauntered off as if he *hadn't* just ripped

Deakin's chest open and squeezed the place where his heart should be. The Stavros he'd known would never have done something like that.

Clear green eyes fastened on his with concern. "He didn't mean it."

"Mean what?"

"Whatever it was that hurt you so badly."

He gave a hard laugh. "It didn't hurt me." It had done something entirely different. "But the Stavros I once knew would have never let himself get that angry."

"You looked pretty mad yourself there for a minute or two. You still do, in fact."

Oh, he'd been beyond mad. If she hadn't physically held his hand in place would he have decked his friend?

Regardless of the fact that he'd been caught by surprise, he hoped not. "So what is your professional opinion? Psychological? Or physiological?"

"I'd say both." Her voice was low. "Something has him extremely upset. And that pinching of his nose is either a terrible headache, pressure from his sinuses, or an overload of stress. It could be something as simple as allergies."

"*Allergies?* Do you find his mood swings consistent with allergies?"

"No, but with the quake you never know what could have been released into the air. A lot of these buildings are hundreds of years old. He could have developed an infection of some type. Or a sensitivity to a toxin. But even if it's none of those things you can't force someone to tell you what's wrong if they really don't want to."

He took a long draw of his whiskey as he studied her face. Hadn't he done that very thing once upon a time? Refused to talk? To anyone? Maybe she'd had experience with patients like him.

"You say that as if you've had that happen before. Did someone refuse to open up to you?"

Her glance skipped away from his for a moment before coming back. "I'm a psychiatrist. I've seen it happen a lot on a professional level."

Why had she emphasized the word 'professional?'

"And on a personal one?"

He had no idea why he'd asked that. He'd have been backpedaling like crazy if she'd asked him to explain Stavros's comment about his father.

He half expected her to get mad, but she didn't.

She just said, "I think we've all experienced that on a personal level from time to time—when you wish you could have helped someone who just didn't want to be helped."

Yes, Lea could definitely be talking about him back in the day. When his parents had insisted he talk to someone he'd clammed up even tighter.

He still didn't like talking about what had happened. To anyone. Not even his closest friends. So who was he to try to force Stavros to open up about whatever was bothering him? What would he have done if the roles were reversed? Probably the very same thing.

So he needed to let this go. If Stavros wanted help he would ask for it. At least he hoped he would. Until then Deakin needed to be available, as a listening ear or a shoulder to cry on. If and when Stavros was ready.

He tossed back the rest of his drink, noting that Lea's was only half gone. He was tempted to order another whiskey, but he was driving—and besides, he somehow doubted Stavros would skip back over to them as if nothing had happened.

"I'm ready if you are." She pushed her drink away from her.

"There's no rush. Go ahead and finish."

"I'm good. I'm kind of a lightweight where

alcohol is concerned." She turned to look across the bar at where Stavros was helping another customer. "Do you want to try to talk him into coming to the clinic and getting checked out?"

"I don't think now is a good time. Maybe when he and I have both had time to cool off."

He glanced around, surprised by how many people were still in the bar this late.

Turning back toward her, he caught her looking at something on the side of his—

Dammit! He didn't want her looking at that. "What are you staring at?"

He'd never called someone out on their curiosity before, but something about the way those green eyes touched his skin had his blood gumming up his veins in a way that was all too familiar.

"Just wondering how you got those."

She seemed unfazed by his challenge. And there was no need to ask what "those" she was talking about. But he wanted to discuss that just about as much as Stavros wanted to talk about what was going on with his health.

Deakin wasn't used to people directly asking him what had happened. He didn't want to tell her and he had no idea why.

Maybe because she was the only person around who didn't have some kind of preconceived idea of who he was or what he had done. The memory of her teeth sinking into her lower lip that first time she'd studied him flickered behind his eyelids. His blood thickened even more, the drumming of it growing in his ears.

"Deakin?"

Only when her voice came again did he realize how much time had passed since she'd asked her original question about his burns.

Her eyes were no longer on his neck, but wholly focused on his face—with an intensity that made his chest burn.

"I got them in a fire."

Like the one beginning to ignite in certain regions below...

Cool fingers touched his hand as he continued to hold her gaze, trying to swallow back his unexpected response to her. He had no idea what had caused it. Or what it was going to take to put it out.

But right now he didn't care. He flipped his hand over to grasp hers, saw her thick lashes sweeping down when he tightened his hold.

And sure as the day was long, those white teeth began to worry at her bottom lip. Back and forth they scrubbed, until his nerve-endings stretched tighter and tighter.

The noise in the room faded to black. His

focus remained glued to her mouth. Her teeth came off, her lips barely parting as if inviting him to peek at the wonders inside.

His will to resist evaporated into thin air.

He leaned forward. The scent of strawberries clung to her. He'd bet she tasted just like that drink. Only better.

When her lashes lifted and her fingers traced across the back of his hand he knew he was done for. It was darker than sin in here. Who would see?

His hand lifted, his fingers threading through the hair at her nape. Then he moved in to see if he was right. One touch was all it would take.

"You want me to add those drinks to your tab, Deak?"

Stavros's strident voice froze him in place, before breaking through his mental fog. He reeled back on his barstool, his hand sliding out of her hair in a rush.

Lea's soft gasp made his teeth clench together.

Dammit. What was wrong with him?

The fact that he didn't *have* a tab would have been funny, except that his friend's timing was even more laughable. There was no longer any anger in the *taverna* owner's face, and Deakin found his attention once more on Stavros's mercurial moods.

A coincidence? No. The very rare times that he'd seen his friend angry, he'd stayed that way.

When he glanced back at Lea she was no longer looking at him, but seemed lost in the drink she'd discarded moments earlier. She drew it back toward her and took a long draw on the straw.

He smiled, feeling as shell-shocked as she looked. Since he was currently wishing he still had part of his drink left in front of him, he couldn't blame her. Maybe she didn't realize just how close he'd come to kissing her.

She took another quick sip, looking anywhere but at him.

Or maybe she did realize.

Someone staring at his scars was normally met with impatience. Or irritation. Not lust. And that was what it had been. An explosive, unexpected tightening of body parts and emotions.

On his part, anyway.

Right now, though, he couldn't worry about any of that. Not with Stavros still perched in front of him.

"Since when do you let anyone put a drink on a tab?"

"The earthquake changed quite a few things."

Yes, it had. It had kept Lea on the island longer than she'd planned. And it had brought him back there and made him want to kiss someone who was a perfect stranger.

"Never mind. I'll just pay for it."

He reached for his wallet, a grimace forming when Lea reached in her own purse.

He stopped her with a look. "Consider this a thank-you for consulting on that patient with me."

Her eyes widened slightly, but she didn't argue. "I was happy to do it."

Stavros had no idea they were talking about him—or if he did he didn't acknowledge that he might be acting out of sorts. "Do you want anything else?"

He certainly did. But he wasn't getting it. Or even asking for it. He was going to go home and take a very cold shower.

Except he needed to give Lea a ride back to the cottage before he could do that. Or he could just take her back to the clinic and let her get on her bike...

He ruled that option out in an instant, and he wasn't sure why.

"I don't." He looked at her. "Do you?"

"No, I think I've had plenty, thanks." She set her drink down, and this time there was a finality to the move that said she was done. Probably in more ways than one.

How angry would Theo be if he ran their newest physician off before he'd even been home a week? Pretty mad, probably—which meant he owed her an apology.

And what if she *hadn't* realized what his intentions were?

Oh, she knew, Deakin, there's no mistaking that.

Which made it even more difficult.

Handing Stavros a bill without bothering to look at it, he said, "Keep the rest."

"Okay!"

Stavros smiled and pocketed the money without bothering to write anything on the receipt. Which was about as strange as his mood swings. His buddy was normally a stickler for keeping his accounts clean and above-board. He'd seen the man stress over not being able to account for ten cents, much less a fifty-euro bill.

Maybe it was like Stavros had said. The earthquake had changed a few things. Even though Deakin had not been there the day it had struck, could it be that the quake was affecting *him* as well? Inducing some kind of mass hysteria?

And that near miss of a kiss? Was that a result of that same mass hysteria?

He had no idea, but the sooner he got out of here the better. Before it set in again and he did something he really would regret.

The man had actually *apologized* to her in the parking lot as they'd sat in the car.

The sting of humiliation was as fresh now as it had been a few nights ago, when he'd driven her home in near silence. She would have sworn he was going to kiss her in the bar, and evidently he'd thought so too, since he'd felt the need to say he was sorry for his actions.

Well, what about *her* actions? She was the one who'd put her hand over his. It had started out as a quick squeeze of comfort, but that had all changed very swiftly.

Then just like that, so had Deakin.

She felt nauseous and out of her depth. Talk about mood swings. And he thought *Stavros* was the one having problems! She needed to keep a level head here and make no mistakes.

Her fiancé had been moody and out of sorts for the last couple of weeks of his life. She'd been worried he was getting cold feet about marrying her.

It had turned out he was. But rather than being specifically about her, his cold feet had been related to living his life—to living in general.

And, while she hadn't completely missed the signs, she'd misread the reasons for them. She'd been just about to break off their engagement in an effort to take some of the pressure off him when he'd died.

Her cellphone rang, making her drop the tube of mascara she'd dug out of her make-up bag. She glanced at the readout. A single name flashed there: *Deakin.*

Ugh! Had he somehow sensed she was thinking about him? In the week since he'd arrived she'd been doing more than her share of that. His transformation from scruffy but breathtaking stranger to clean-shaven, competent doctor had put her off balance and kept her off balance ever since.

No, that wasn't true. She'd been off balance since the first day he'd strolled into the clinic in all his scruffy glory.

Her thumb hovered over the answer button.

Maybe he was going to tell her she was no longer welcome to use his bicycle. Or, worse, that he wanted her to move out of the cottage. Had the hotel she'd been staying at opened up? She didn't think she could afford to stay there long-term, since she wasn't being paid an actual salary at the clinic. *Yet.*

She blinked as the phone rang for the third time. Was she hoping she *would* be paid at some point? That Theo would ask her to stay on the island?

Had what had happened with Deakin changed her mind about Mythelios? No. It hadn't. She still loved it. Just as much if not more than she had before.

Taking a deep, reassuring breath, she pushed the "receive call" button on the phone just as it was getting ready to send the caller to voice-mail.

"Hello."

"You knew it was me."

Since her greeting hadn't had a question mark at the end of it, it was kind of a given.

"I did. As we're working together, I figured I'd better enter your name into my contacts. In case of an emergency."

And it would come right out again once one of them left the island.

There was a pause.

"Right."

A few more empty seconds ticked by. Just when she thought the connection had broken, his voice came back.

"I have to make a boat-run to Naxos for some supplies. With the stores here still sustaining damage, and since the airstrip is barely able to handle traffic, we're running short of a few things at the clinic—and here at the house as well."

She had no idea why he was telling her this. Was he asking if there was anything she needed? If so, he wasn't doing a very good job of it.

"Okay…"

She let the end of the word trail on long enough to let him know she was confused. At least she hoped it came across that way.

"Would you like to go with me?"

She'd started to rattle off a generic answer before his words actually registered. "I'm sorry?"

"I asked if you wanted to go with me. Theo says you've been working round the clock and that neither he nor Cailey have been able to see their way free to give you a tour of the neighboring islands."

He paused again.

"I didn't realize you'd been working non-stop for all this time with no pay. That has to be remedied."

"It's okay. I've enjoyed it—even though I'm not happy about the reason for it."

"Having your vacation cut short by an earthquake is probably *not* on Mythelios's list of local attractions."

Was that a smile she heard in his voice? "It isn't. Not in the tour book I looked at, anyway."

"Well, I'm sure Theo, myself and the other partners will meet at some point and discuss things. We'll reimburse you for all your help, of course."

Just when she'd thought he was offering to be her tour guide on a fun outing his real motives for wanting her to go made themselves known. He felt guilty that she hadn't been paid.

Her tummy sank through the floor. So much for that smile.

Theo had offered to pay her early on, and she'd turned him down. But now, after more than a month, her savings account was beginning to show signs of strain, even though she didn't have the expense of a hotel. She still had food and supplies of her own to buy.

"So, do you want to go with me? We should have some time to sightsee a little bit. Are you interested in archeology at all?"

"I love it."

Despite her misgivings over his reasons for asking, something in the low rumble of his voice cast a spell over her and made her want to go with him wherever he wanted. Or at least keep him on the phone for a little while longer.

"I haven't even gotten to see the ruins on Mythelios yet, let alone the other islands."

"Hmm…"

A strange tingling went to work in her midsection. Had that dark shadow crept back across his jawline since she'd last seen him? Was his new shorter hair sticking up at odd angles? Her eyes closed as she tried to draw up an image of just that. Maybe he was still shirtless. Or…even better…lying in bed, one arm propped behind his head as he talked to her, with only a sheet covering his—

Lordy! You need to stop that.

The tingling grew into something a little more volatile. A lot more dangerous. She hadn't fantasized about a man since Mark's death. If she wasn't careful all her self-lectures regarding nice, uncomplicated guys were going to fly out the window. Deakin was definitely not "uncomplicated". Not by any stretch of the imagination. And neither were her current reactions to him.

She shouldn't go. Should she…?

"How long would we be gone?"

Well, okay… Her subconscious had evidently disconnected itself and gone rogue.

But he was right. She hadn't had much of a break in weeks, and when she thought about it she *was* pretty drained. Not tired enough to quit and leave the island, but in the rush of those first couple of weeks of emergencies at the clinic she hadn't really had time to stop and think about her own needs. And here Deakin was, offering to change all that. If she'd let him.

But was it smart? Especially given her thoughts a few seconds ago.

Probably not. It was getting harder and harder to view him as a simple colleague. Especially after that encounter in the bar, when she'd been so sure he was going to kiss her.

Now that he'd held out the offer, however, she was going to have a very hard time turning him down, no matter what his motives were.

"We can play it by ear and see as little or as much as you want. The Cyclades form a rough circle around the island of Delos, a sacred site in these parts. It's not inhabited, but it is open to the public during certain hours. We could see the sights and then have lunch on the boat—in the air-conditioning if it gets too hot."

Her brows went up and she pressed the phone a little closer to her ear. "Your boat is air-conditioned?"

"It was my dad's boat, but yes."

His dad's? His parents were both dead. Deakin had surely inherited the boat. So why didn't he think of it as his? Grief? Was it a reminder of his mom and dad? Or maybe it was like the main house. He just hadn't put his stamp of ownership on it yet.

"Are you sure they'll be okay at the clinic without us?"

"I'm sure between Theo, Cailey, Petra and the rest of the staff they'll be just fine. I did let Theo know about the results of our visit to Stavros. Hopefully he'll change his mind and come in to see us."

She could almost hear his mental shrug. "Do you think he will? Maybe I should stay behind just in case."

"Stavros is pretty stubborn. But we'll only be an hour away, in any case, if he does—or if an emergency comes up that they can't handle, Theo can easily call us back in."

The way he'd asked all the partners after the earthquake? She knew that Theo had tried to contact Chris, Ares and Deakin and had asked them to come back, but so far only Deakin had answered that call and that had taken a little over a month. She knew that work obligations made it very hard, but it had been tough in those first days, trying to juggle panicked earthquake victims and their families.

A lump formed in her throat.

Maybe it would do her some good to get away from the island for a while. It might even help her shake off the sense of guilt and sadness over Mark's death that followed her like the caboose on a long, noisy train. A caboose that followed her everywhere, no matter how hard she tried to outrun it.

With that, her decision was made.

"Well, since seeing the islands was one of the reasons I came to Mythelios in the first place, I would love to go. Thank you."

"You're welcome. Theo has been after me to make sure you see a thing or two while I'm home."

Her stomach, which had just started creeping back to its normal resting place, went into freefall all over again.

"Please don't feel obligated to take me."

She hated the way her voice came out, small and uncertain. But that was how she felt.

A beat or two went by. "I don't, and I'm sorry if it sounded that way. I would have asked you to come whether Theo had suggested it or not. I already promised to take you out on the boat, didn't I? It just made sense to combine business with pleasure."

Pleasure? Oh, the sightseeing portion of the trip.

"It does. And I'm sure I'll love Delos as much as I do Mythelios."

And she did love Mythelios.

She loved the mixture of quaint and sophisticated that was a normal part of life here. And it even helped her understand her parents a little better. They had always been so insistent on following tradition. She had thought the mix of old-fashioned Greek beliefs with living in a modern foreign city was strange when she was a teenager. But she was learning that the very texture of Greek society seemed to be the same way: holding fast to tradition while embracing all things new.

She could hardly believe she'd arrived only a few weeks ago. In some ways it felt as if she'd been here for years.

"Do you?"

It took her a minute to realize he was commenting on her statement about loving Mythelios. He sounded puzzled, as if he had no idea what she found so attractive about the island. Maybe he was inured to the charm of the place.

"I really do. Who wouldn't?"

"You might be surprised."

She moved the phone to her other ear. "You don't?"

"I don't *hate* it."

Said as if there had been a time when he had…

She decided to change the subject in case he decided to argue the point. "I'm glad. What time do you want to leave?"

"Anytime you're ready."

"As in now?"

Ack! She still needed to shower and change. Ducking down, she grabbed the tube of mascara she'd dropped a few minutes earlier and did a quick set of calculations.

"Can you give me about twenty-five minutes?"

"How about an hour? That way I can pick up some things for lunch. Unless you're rather eat on Delos? I have to warn you it'll be hot."

"I'm getting use to the heat, and eating on the boat sounds heavenly. Do you want me to bring anything?"

"Just some sunscreen…and yourself."

With that, he hung up, leaving her looking at the phone in consternation. She *would* bring herself. But it wouldn't be the self who was currently crushing over a certain Dr. Patera.

An hour later she was showered and ready in a white floral sundress and comfy espadrilles. And, judging from Deakin's double-take, she looked a little different out of the casual clinic wear he normally saw her in. Speaking of which… She needed to get another set of scrubs if she was planning on staying for much longer. Her current set was on loan from Cailey, and she really needed one of her own.

How much longer *was* she staying?

She smiled and closed the front door of the cottage. That was something she didn't need to worry about. At least not today.

"I'm glad you wore something cool. It'll be warm. Especially on Delos, if we arrive during the heat of the day."

When else would they be arriving? She had no idea what the maritime rules were for Mythelios, but it might not be wise to be stuck out on the water with Deakin at night. Under a full moon.

Wise for whom? *Her?*

She made an internal scoffing sound. This was not going to be a romantic trip. It was a business outing. He'd as much as said that. Yes, but he'd also said they were going to be combining business with pleasure. She was the one who'd placed special emphasis on the second half of that statement.

The boat house—a tall white structure with a cupola perched over it—had always fascinated her. She'd actually never stepped inside the building. With its black weather vane twisting and turning at each change in the breeze, it had a very nautical feel to it.

Deakin unlocked the door and threw it open, letting a sliver of light into the dark space. A large form rose and fell, and then, with the flip of a light switch, the ghost was gone, replaced with a sleek ship.

Mytheliostocracy II.

She blinked a time or two at the black name emblazoned on the side of the boat. It seemed kind of…pretentious. Like the house across the gardens.

She frowned, then hurried to erase the expression before Deakin saw her reaction. It wasn't disappointment. It was just…surprise.

Deakin didn't fit. With any of it. Especially not the shaggy-haired version of the man she'd met that first day. Maybe that was why he'd said it was his father's boat. He didn't want to be linked with this kind of lifestyle. Maybe that was also why Deakin traveled from place to place, trying to help relieve suffering in other countries. It was a way to physically remove himself from what it represented.

Which was what? Wealth? Extravagance? Deakin wasn't exactly poor, though. From what she'd heard he, Theo and the other two, Ares and Chris, had joined funds to pay for the running of the clinic year after year once Theo's father had made the initial investment to open it.

Mytheliostocracy II matched the color of the building it was housed in, but all resemblance began and ended there. The boathouse was traditional. The vessel ultramodern. A strange mixture, to be sure.

Just like the clinic. Just like the island. Just like Deakin...?

No, he was traditional through and through. He looked and sounded Greek, but he didn't really seem to feel comfortable in the house—or on Mythelios, for that matter. Or was that just her imagination?

She shifted the large bag she was carrying over her shoulder, and Deakin seemed to shake himself out of some kind of trance.

He took the satchel from her. "Anything you need in here right away?"

"I have some sunscreen I'll need to eventually get to, but I can put that on later."

"Let me show you around and then we'll cast off."

He stepped from the solid expanse of the dock to the vessel's surface, which rocked slightly under his weight. Holding onto one of the railings, he reached for her hand. She grabbed it before hopping across herself.

The deck was made of some kind of light polished wood. It gleamed under the lights. Like the cottage and the house, it looked as if it was cleaned regularly. Another thing Deakin's aunt took care of?

"Why don't you visit the island more often?"

The question came out of nowhere, and she immediately wished she hadn't asked. But it was too late to retract the words.

"I'm busy with my own career."

"Do you only work with one relief organization?"

"For the most part, yes."

If he was upset by the question, he didn't show it, just moved across the deck and motioned her to follow. He gestured up a set of short steps that led to an area perched over the bow which housed a wheel and gear levers. Lots of them.

"That's where we drive it."

"We?"

"Surely you want to try it out?" One side of his mouth kicked up.

"I don't know. It looks very complicated."

"Once you get used to it, it's not that bad."

Kind of like Deakin…

He went down another set of stairs until he reached a door on the left. "This is the kitchen."

Small, but well-equipped, the kitchen had a refrigerator and a stove with several burners. The drawers probably housed pots and pans and other essential items. Deakin crouched in front of the small fridge and unloaded the bag of items he'd brought. Meat and cheese, water, soft drinks. And beer. She smiled at that. Not a very aristocratic beverage.

"How did the boat get its name?"

"Mytheliostocracy?"

She nodded. "I take it that wasn't your idea?"

"No. I think my dad saw his company as the aristocracy of the island. He combined that with Mythelios and came up with the name."

It made sense, but it still seemed like an odd thing to name a boat.

"Oh."

"You don't like it?" He propped his hips against the countertop, long legs stretching across to the other side of the galley.

The space suddenly seemed small. And close. She wouldn't be able to get past him without climbing over his legs—and, depending on which way she faced, either her boobs or her butt would brush against him as she went.

She gulped.

"It's not for me to like or dislike," she managed.

Was it a little hard to breathe down here with the windows shut? Or was it just because every time she inhaled his warm scent filled her lungs and trickled through her bloodstream until it reached her heart, making her pulse race?

The scars on his jaw and neck that he seemed

to hate so much did nothing to diminish her reaction to him. It was raw and vital and she wanted nothing better than to bury her visceral response to him deep underground, where it could no longer reach her.

She did the next best thing: tried to prompt him into moving to another location. "So, what other goodies does this old barge have on it?"

He grinned, but pushed away from the counter. "Old barge, huh? That about sums it up."

It didn't. Not at all. But it made her realize something.

"You don't like the name your dad chose for the boat."

"Not particularly."

Her brows went up at how quickly the words had come out of his mouth. "The boat is yours now. Why not change it?"

"I don't consider it mine. Not really. And I haven't changed it because it's what the first one was named."

"The first one?"

"It doesn't matter." He frowned. "I'm not here often enough to go through the trouble of having it repainted. Let me finish showing you around so we can get underway."

He took her to a small powder room, and then to an area at the front of the boat where she could sun herself. *Yeah, right.* She glanced up to where the control room was. Any sun-bathing would be done under the watchful eye of whoever was steering the boat.

She shivered at the thought of Deakin look-ing at her almost naked body.

That wasn't happening.

Good thing she hadn't brought a suit.

"And here are the sleeping quarters."

He opened the last door at the end of the nar-row hallway and the opulence suddenly ended. The bed was big and impressive, yes, but the furnishings were not. A simple cotton bed-spread was tossed over the bed. There was a lamp. A braided rug on the floor. And a night-stand on either side of the bed.

This was probably where Deakin spent the majority of his time when on the boat. She couldn't see whoever had named the boat choosing such spartan décor. But it fit Dea-kin to a tee. His need for simplicity. Especially after traveling the world and seeing its poverty first hand. So why hadn't he made the same transformation with the main house?

"I like it."

He smiled. "Better than the name?"

"Much better." She echoed his smile and raised him one. "This looks comfortable. A space you could actually enjoy being in."

Only after she'd said it did she realize how it

had sounded. Her daydream from earlier that morning came back to haunt her with a vengeance. The one that had had Deakin lying on a bed as he talked to her. He'd been totally naked, a sheet covering his bottom half. And the sheet had been thin enough that she could make out his form beneath it…the strong legs which came together to form a triangle. And topping that had been a telltale bulge… One that had stirred even as she'd looked at it.

She was suddenly glancing at anything *but* that bed. God, if he knew what she'd been imagining…

"Okay, so where to next?"

The panic flooding her system made its way into her voice. And when she met Deakin's gaze his smile was long gone.

Deakin backed out of the door. "Anywhere but here."

With those enigmatic words he turned and headed toward the main deck.

And safety.

CHAPTER FIVE

"Deakin! So glad you came. Would you mind looking at a patient for me before you pick up the things Theo requested?"

Konstantinos Banis, an older doctor who had worked on Naxos for many years, met them at the front elevators at the clinic.

"Of course."

Like himself, Dr. Banis was a plastic surgeon specializing in burns. In fact the man had been here when Deakin was brought in as a teen, his skin charred and weeping after the explosion that had almost cost him his life.

Ville had been treated back on Mythelios, so he'd been the one to recount the story of what had happened.

Or his version of it.

Deakin had only heard it months later in Athens, after he was through the worst of his surgeries. He'd just let it stand. After all, Deakin had been the one to strike that match. And

Ville had had much more to lose if the truth came out.

Dr. Banis had followed his case long after he'd left his care and his clinic, coming to visit him through years of skin grafts. The two were now friends. He was also the only person in the world except for Deakin and Ville who knew the whole truth—and that was only because his young patient had muttered odd phrases while delirious with pain. He'd put two and two together and confronted him.

Neither boy had been charged with any crime, so Dr. Banis had also let things stand as that was what Deakin had wanted.

Deakin didn't care about any of that right now. He was still half regretting inviting Lea along for the ride. Yes, Theo had suggested he take her, but Deakin had already invited her to join him on the water soon after they'd met.

Was it so that his normal "penance cruise" could be postponed? He'd never brought anyone with him on one before. And the spartan nature of the bedroom that Lea liked so much was because he didn't consider these trips pleasure cruises. They were to remind himself of the consequences of poor choices and of allowing peer pressure to overrule common sense.

Some of those consequences he carried on

his person. And some of them he carried in his head.

His decisions had affected his parents for years afterwards. He never wanted that kind of responsibility to hang over his head ever again. He could have told his dad the truth, but the chilly relationship they'd shared wouldn't have changed.

"Could I come as well?"

Lea's voice broke through his brooding. Another reminder that bringing her might have been a mistake. Because as he'd stood behind her in that bedroom he'd wanted to sweep her up into his arms and drop her onto the bed and do some very un-aristocratic things to her.

He glanced at Konstantinos, who nodded. "It's fine by me."

Better do the introductions, then. He'd hoped to get in, get the supplies, make a quick run to Delos and be home before anything disastrous had a chance to happen.

"Lea Risi, this is Dr. Banis, who also works with burn patients."

He omitted the rest of it, afraid that it might open the door for Konstantinos to talk about Deakin's injuries. And the reasons for them.

The two shook hands. "I take it you're a doctor as well?"

"Yes. I'm in psychiatry—specializing in PTSD treatments."

"PTSD?" The other man sent Deakin a sharp look.

"For the earthquake victims," he clarified, hoping Lea wouldn't read anything into Konstantinos's speculative tone.

Except she had. Her head had that funny little tilt it got when she was trying to puzzle through something.

How did he even *know* that?

"Of course," the other doctor answered, patting Deakin on the shoulder.

Dammit. Why did everyone assume that he had some kind of deep-rooted issues related to his accident?

No, don't answer that.

"What is the issue with your patient?"

"Let's walk and I'll tell you."

They headed up the corridor of the Ierá Lytrotís Clinic. It was much different from their own clinic in that this place was the epitome of efficiency at the expense of comfort. Not that one was any better than the other. They just focused on different priorities.

A few minutes later they stood in front of a patient's door while Konstantinos gave them the rundown on his injuries. "I'm thinking about care-flighting him just like I did—"

"Why care-flight?" Deakin interrupted, even though he didn't care one whit about whether or not he would send this patient to Athens. He'd just been trying to cut his old doctor off before he finished the rest of that sentence, because he knew exactly how the man had planned to end it: *Just like I did with you.*

Why was he so desperate to keep Lea from knowing what had happened to him?

Was it really because she was the one person on Mythelios who was untainted by public opinion?

"Well, Athens sees a lot more of this type of case than we do."

Deakin pushed aside his own issues. "Is the patient critical?"

"Not at the moment, but with third-degree burns massive infection is always a possibility. I'll need you both to scrub up and wear protective gear while you're in there."

"Understood. Where can we do that?"

"Just inside the door. We already have a negative pressure room set up beyond that area."

Deakin's brows went up. "That's a new addition."

"Yes. We only had to do about twenty fundraisers to make it happen."

"Did you do a bachelor auction?"

Dr. Banis frowned. "A what?"

"Never mind—it was a joke."

Kind of like the calendar had been. But, hey, it had actually brought in some much-needed money. If the auction could do the same thing, maybe even get that CT machine they needed, then it would be worth it. Maybe he should let them auction him off after all…

Lea, who had been quiet during the walk to the room, spoke up. "Is counseling offered to burn patients on a regular basis?"

The hair on the back of Deakin's neck stood up. Why had she asked that question?

"Not normally, but if the resultant scars are disfiguring, or we feel the patient's quality of life will be affected at all, we might refer that patient to a psychiatrist."

"Okay. I just wondered… Because burns—especially third-degree burns—can cause mental anguish in addition to the physical injuries. Lives sometimes change dramatically."

"Yes, they do."

The murmured words were out of Deakin's mouth before he could shut them down. He was speaking in general terms. Wasn't he? But when both pairs of eyes shifted to him he knew they had taken them as a commentary on his own life.

And they'd be right.

"All the more reason to talk to an objective party about the experience and receive support," Lea said.

"And some people prefer to keep private matters private," he snapped.

If he'd hoped that would stop the direction of this conversation in its tracks, he'd been wrong. Lea's face darkened, color seeping into her cheeks in a way that said she was angry.

"Even if that choice has a devastating effect on those around you?"

Whoa. Wait a minute. His decision not to talk to a counselor had been the choice of a kid who was embarrassed and ashamed of what his actions had cost his parents financially. And about how they had changed his looks— something that was foremost on most teenagers' minds. But as far as *devastating* anyone went…that definitely hadn't happened.

He looked closer at the flashing eyes and trembling chin and realized that the anger she was feeling wasn't directed at him. At least not specifically. Then who?

Someone she knew in a personal sense?

Time to shift topic.

"Of course not. And Dr. Banis is right to encourage people to seek help. But you can't force anyone to talk about their problems. Just like a certain someone we visited the other day."

Lea pulled in a deep breath and then let it blow out. "Sorry. I just get passionate about my job sometimes."

Dr. Banis gave Deakin's shoulder a quick squeeze. "As do we all. Now, shall we go see the patient I was talking about?"

And just like that the storm was over. At least for now. The situation told him one thing, though. He was going to have to watch what he said once they got into that patient's room.

Burn patients always affected him, even though he dealt with them all the time. His profession often transported him back to a place he would just as soon forget. If he wasn't careful Lea might learn all the secrets he'd worked so hard to keep anyone from discovering.

And, if what he sensed was true, the beautiful psychiatrist might just have a secret or two of her own…

They opened the door, the slight hiss of air as they went through designed to keep microbes from coming in. In the bed was an unconscious fifty-nine-year-old man, his face swathed in bandages that covered everything—even his eyes.

"What was the temperature of the grease?"

The patient had been injured by high-temperature grease in a huge industrial vat. He'd slipped on a mat while leaning over to add chicken to the fryer and his face had been dunked below the surface for a second before he'd come up screaming.

His old friend checked the chart and read off the figure.

Deakin swore softly under his breath. Hot enough to sear meat on contact. "His eyes?"

Konstantinos shook his head.

Hell. At least Deakin had retained his sight. "He's in an induced coma at the moment."

The surgeon showed him before-and-after pictures—one of what the man had looked like before the accident, and one after he'd been debrided for the first time. The difference was staggering. In the first picture the man, Elias, had a youthful salt-and-pepper look to him, his smile brightening his whole face. A face that was now unrecognizable.

"His airway isn't affected, but we put a trach tube in to make it easier to treat the facial burns."

Deakin had never felt fortunate to have had the burns he had, but at this moment he saw life through the eyes of this patient and swallowed. If he survived it was going to be tough, but as long as he had a good support group, unlike *he'd* had, he would make it through.

And this man's injuries weren't due to stupidity. It had been a senseless accident. Something that could have happened to anyone.

"Does he have a family?"

"Yes. He doesn't have children, but his wife has been here almost nonstop. I had to order her to go home and get some rest. She should be back again in a few hours."

"Do you already have a grafting team set up?"

Konstantinos fixed Deakin with a speculative stare. "I'm working on the best plastic surgeon I know right now."

Deakin shook his head. "I won't be around when he's ready to start reconstructive surgery."

From the way Lea's head swiveled his way, he guessed she was shocked to hear that. She shouldn't be. The whole island knew that Deakin never stuck around for long.

Except she wasn't an islander. Was she relieved he'd be leaving soon?

"How about counseling for him and probably his wife too? Will *you* 'be around', Dr. Risi?"

"I'm not sure, yet."

This man wouldn't be ready to talk about his hopes and fears for months. Did Lea really think she might still be on the island by then?

His friend sighed. "Maybe I *should* care-flight him to Athens, then. I have a good team here, but not enough to give him the twenty-four-hour care he needs. The problem is that his wife is a nurse here at the clinic, and we'll really have a hard time replacing her if he goes—she'll want to be with him as much as possible."

If he'd hoped to guilt Deakin into staying he was going to be disappointed, even though he doubted Konstantino was really trying to do that.

"I'm sorry. I can take a copy of the chart and read over it—give you my recommendations if that would help."

"It would indeed, thank you, Deak. I'll be looking forward to hearing your opinion."

A few minutes later they were on their way. But first Deakin made a quick trip to the restroom, leaning over the sink to splash water onto his face. He'd dealt with some pretty horrific burns during his career, but...*damn*.

And Lea... Something about the possibility of her remaining on the island really bothered him. He couldn't put a finger on exactly why, but there was a niggling in his gut that wouldn't go away.

But it would eventually. Once he was off the island and on his way back to Africa, or wherever they sent him next.

At least he hoped so. Because otherwise he was in a lot of trouble.

And so were his patients if he couldn't get his head screwed back on straight. So he would just work hard to make sure that happened. No matter what it took.

The ruins rose from the earth, their white stone catching the mid-morning sun and creating a dazzling display visible even from their position on the water. It gave Delos an ethereal, magical feel.

Lea glanced over at where Deakin was manning the wheel and saw his face was aimed at the shoreline as well. His shoulders were more relaxed than she had seen them all day. Actually, since their very first meeting back at the clinic on Mythelios.

With sunglasses hiding his dark eyes, she'd had no way of knowing what he was thinking until now, when his psyche seemed to breathe a huge sigh of relief.

He liked it here.

Coming had been the right decision, although after their tense back-and-forth exchange at the clinic on Naxos she had been kicking herself for agreeing to the trip.

His words about some people preferring to keep private matters private had touched a nerve and she'd erupted. Something she rarely did. But suicide was never a "private" matter. *Ever*. Who knew that better than she did?

But she needed to let it go. This was not about Mark. Not anymore. And if she couldn't move beyond it she was going to need to talk to someone herself. She had no right to criticize Deakin for something she had caught herself doing time and time again since Mark had died: bottling up her pain.

It had also bothered her when Deakin had been so quick to say that he wouldn't be around when that burn patient needed surgery. Wasn't there *anything* he would miss about Mythelios?

"We're getting close. Do you want to take the wheel for a few minutes? I should have asked you earlier."

Even his voice sounded more content.

"I'm good. Just enjoying my first glimpse of the island." Perched on the seat next to his in the small wheelhouse, she admired the view again. "It's beautiful. It's hard to believe a place like this actually exists outside of books."

"Yes. I'm glad the island has remained uninhabited except for some essential staff."

"Mainland Greece has ruins, but I haven't seen any of the ones on the islands."

"Most of them have some. Mythelios has an Apollo's Temple and a few other ruins."

"I'd heard about the temple, but with the earthquake I haven't gotten a chance to explore much past the village where the clinic is."

"I'm surprised Petra hasn't taken you."

"She's had a lot on her plate, with the clinic and visiting her mom. I don't think she has much down time."

"Hmm…"

She had no idea what that meant. But if she'd been expecting him to offer to drive her around on a sightseeing tour of his home island she was sorely mistaken. Not that she did. Expect him to do that, that was. It was enough to have the day off to enjoy.

She hadn't realized the exhausting pace she'd been keeping until getting on this boat, actually. She'd found her head lolling a couple of times as she sat beside Deakin. Especially since he'd been so quiet for most of the trip.

He hadn't said anything about it. Maybe he hadn't even noticed her head jerking from time to time. Or maybe he'd been grateful for it. It meant he hadn't needed to keep her company.

"Do you want to eat an early lunch first and then go to the island? We have time if you want to lie down for a little while below."

Her face heated. So he *had* noticed. "Sorry. It's been a little chaotic on Mythelios over the last few weeks. I'm more tired than I realized."

He slowed the boat until the engines barely throbbed. The vibrations rattled her stomach as he turned in his seat to look at her.

"It's the letdown from adrenaline. I get it too. After I've been dealing with tragedies in other countries I feel like I could sleep for a week."

"Yes. I feel that way now. But I want to explore the island first. I can sleep later."

"You can nap on the way back to Mythelios, if you want. It's not a long trip, but I can draw it out a little. There's nothing like sleeping on the water."

Said as if he did that a lot. Maybe he did…

"You must love having your dad's boat."

"I don't think 'love' is the right word. I've been thinking of selling it, actually."

"Why?" If she lived on Mythelios and had something like this she would be out on the water every chance she got.

"I'm rarely on the island anymore. If it weren't for the clinic I'd probably sell the house too, and relocate completely."

That she could understand. She'd stayed in Toronto after Mark had died because of her job and that whole thing about not making radical decisions in the midst of a crisis. She'd held on to her job and the apartment for probably longer than she should have.

Living on Mythelios had showed her that she was ready to move on and hopefully leave the past where it belonged. The heartache would always be there. But hopefully it wouldn't be as sharp and painful after a few years.

"Does it hurt living in your parents' house, surrounded by their memories?"

It took him a minute to answer. "It's uncomfortable at times."

She thought he was going to add something else, but he didn't. "Do you have a practice somewhere else? Or do you only do relief work?"

"I've done short stints on several of the islands, including Naxos and in Athens. I'm beginning to think I'm a nomad at heart, though."

"No thoughts of marriage or kids?"

He gave her a sharp look. "No."

Oh, Lord, had he thought she was applying for the position? Nothing could be farther from the truth.

"I was engaged, but it didn't work out, so I see where you're coming from." The words came out of a place of injured pride—just to show him that she wasn't some desperate teenager hoping for her first kiss.

"I'm sorry. Was he in medicine too?"

"Yes. He was a doctor."

Deakin shut off the engines and hit a button.

A rumble from somewhere underneath them had her frowning.

"Just setting the anchor." He swiveled his chair toward her and propped his sunglasses on top of his head, looking at her face. "Is that why you left Toronto? A broken engagement?"

"We didn't break the engagement."

"But you said it didn't work out."

She never should have said anything. But now that she had there was no going back. "He died."

"Oh, hell. Lea, I'm sorry. Was he ill?"

"Yes. He was. Only no one knew it." Suddenly, she knew she was going to tell him. *Needed* to tell him. "He committed suicide six months before our wedding day."

If the words shocked him he didn't let on. He leaned across and wrapped his hand around hers. "What a damned fool."

"Excuse me?" She'd expected sympathy. Pity, even. Not the low angry sentence he'd just gritted out.

"He just left you to deal with the fallout."

"There was something going on inside of him that none of us knew about."

Lea still didn't know what. Mark had left no suicide note, so all she and his family had been able to do was guess as to why he'd done it, which somehow made it even worse.

"He never talked to you about it?"

"No, obviously not. I would have asked him to go see someone."

Deakin's lips tightened slightly, but he only nodded. "I'm sorry to have brought up a painful memory."

"You didn't know. It's why I came to Mythelios, actually. I needed a change of venue. A chance to get away from the apartment we shared and think about everything from a distance."

"Will you go back to Canada?"

"Long-term? I don't know. I will probably have to at some point, though. My folks live there, and since I haven't put out any job applications yet I'll eventually have to start looking. This was supposed to be a vacation. And it's been a good one—despite the earthquake. Or maybe even because of it."

He smiled. "Not exactly *my* idea of a good time."

"Maybe not."

The canopy over the upper part of the boat, provided shade from the brutal sun, and there was a balmy breeze blowing across the water.

She took a deep breath and sighed, looking at his face. "So how do you fit in vacation time since you travel so much?"

"I have a little downtime in between assignments, but work is all the therapy I need."

Who'd said anything about therapy? She'd been talking about holidays. Vacations. Time not spent working. "Everyone should have a way to decompress."

He let go of her hand. "Well, not everyone has access to Serenity Gardens. Sometimes we have to work with the hand we've been dealt in life."

"I like to think we can shuffle our deck and start over with a new hand," she said quietly.

"Is that what this trip was about for you? Reshuffling the deck?" he asked.

She kicked her sandals off and tucked up her feet under her, then rearranged the hem of her sundress so that it covered her legs. "You don't sound like you agree."

"It's not that I disagree, I just don't think you can ever get completely away from the past." He nodded over the surface of the water. "Just like on Delos, there are fragments that remain embedded in us. We can't uproot them, no matter how hard we might try."

"Maybe. But perhaps that's the way it *should* be. Our experiences—good and bad—shape us. Delos wouldn't be the same without those ruins, don't you agree?"

Following her lead, Deakin stretched his

long legs out and crossed his arms over his chest, the muscles in his upper arms tightening. "I'd have to think about it."

That was okay. He didn't have to agree or disagree with her. He had the right to his own opinion. She would never be able to say that Mark's death had been a positive experience. It had been horrific, and she still got angry and sad about what he had done. But there was no changing it.

Her trip was supposed to clear her head and help her decide which direction to take for the next chapter of her life. But fate had intervened and she hadn't gotten the chance to do that yet. Deakin coming home might have forced the issue, though. She couldn't stay in his cottage forever. Maybe it was time for her to start applying at hospitals in Canada and see where it took her.

Vacations were meant to be temporary. This hadn't been a typical getaway, but it had given her a chance to be immersed in medicine—not just psychiatry—and feel truly useful. Maybe she should try to do what Deakin did. Travel from place to place and find work wherever the wind carried her.

Except she liked being settled in one spot. She didn't think she was the world-traveler type. And when she'd arrived on Mythelios there had been a sense of rightness that she'd never felt before. Maybe she could find another place that gave her that same feeling.

Deakin sat up, his sunglasses back in place, as if making a decision. "Well, I'm ready to eat if you are. And then afterwards we'll explore the island."

The little bit of sharing they'd done was evidently over, from the sound of it. This was the quiet, solemn Deakin she'd first met. If she hadn't been there to witness his outburst when he'd learned that Mark had committed suicide she might have doubted it had ever happened.

And the hand-holding?

A temporary detour. Now he was back on a road well-traveled and sparsely populated. And it looked like he was on it to stay.

CHAPTER SIX

DEAKIN SHOULDERED THE knapsack filled with their supplies and hopped from the boat onto the dock before turning to offer Lea his hand. Armed with a floppy white hat that matched her dress—and the island's many pillars—she looked cool and touristy, a very different person from the businesslike woman he'd met in the clinic lobby.

Her warm fingers landed in his, and she held her hat on her head with the other hand as she stepped across. The wind whipped her dress, molding it to her body, making him move uncomfortably before forcing himself to shift his attention to something else.

"Wow, this is amazing! And incredibly windy! I'm glad my hat has a tie."

She took a moment to take it off and pull the ribbons from inside, before knotting them under her chin. Then she gazed around the hills, where the ruins were scattered as if a huge hand had swept across the hilly terrain and sent things flying in different directions.

A large tour group ambled by, cameras at the ready, blocking their view for a minute or two.

She frowned. "Do we have to do the guided thing, or can we look around on our own?"

"Whatever you prefer. I'm familiar with most of the sights, and I have a tour book with me if you want to read more about any specific ruins."

"You came prepared! And, yes, exploring at our leisure would be great."

She trusted him to take her around. That fact shouldn't have sent a flicker of anticipation through him. But it did. He was just as happy to avoid the tourist scene, with up to fifty people all jostling for position to get the best photos. Besides, this way no one would ask awkward questions or assume they were a couple.

Her comment on the boat about reshuffling life's deck of cards had hit him like a ton of bricks. But it wasn't possible. At least not for him. Every time he came to Mythelios and stayed in his parents' house he was reminded of what had happened that day…of what life had been like afterwards. Ville could have been killed, or ended up like Konstantino's patient, and then he would have more than just a boat and a boathouse on his conscience.

The times he felt the most relief were when he pulled out of that boat dock and headed away from the island where he was raised. Like today, coming to Delos with Lea. Then he could be himself, rather than the person he thought everyone saw when they looked at him.

He led the way from the boat ramp, pausing as another large group passed them on the right. Lea's attention was already shifting from place to place, her eyes alight with interest.

The tense muscles in his shoulders relaxed. As much as he hated to admit it, he liked the idea of just the two of them strolling through these ancient areas.

She'd balled up the side of her dress to keep it from blowing up Marilyn Monroe style.

"I thought wearing this was going to keep me cool, but I guess I should have rethought that."

No, she shouldn't. With its spaghetti straps holding up a snug bodice and the skirt flying around her legs, the floral print dress provided a bright spot of color among the white buildings. It was sexy and free, and he liked it a little more than he should have.

More than one guy had glanced their way—

probably wondering what a beauty like this was doing in his company.

He shook off that thought.

"There's not much shade, so let me know if you get too hot. We can take a break and go back to the boat."

"I'm fine for now." She gave a quick smile and flicked the fluttering brim of her hat. "And I brought my own shade…and a built in fan."

"I brought some water and snacks." He shifted the backpack to his other shoulder.

The midsummer heat could crush the most exuberant explorer and send them packing back to their tourist boat—if it was still docked. Another reason to go it on their own. They could easily go back to *Mytheliostocracy II* and cool off for a while.

She nodded. "Let me know if you want me to carry it for a while."

"I'm good, but thanks."

Yet another group came by and someone jostled Lea, almost knocking her over. Deakin grabbed her hand and hauled her close to let them pass. Instead of pulling away, her hand curled around his in a way that was comfortable and familiar. Something else that he liked.

They started up the footpath, past some crumbling buildings. "What are these?"

"This is the residential area. The wealthier

homes had marble floors and pillars. And a built-in bathroom."

"Built in?"

He grinned. "Well, after a fashion. There was no plumbing. Just a trough." He motioned to a long, narrow dug-out section of the floor that was lined with marble stones.

"You're kidding?"

That made him laugh, giving her shoulder a nudge with his. "Not interested in time-traveling back to that era, then?"

"For a visit? Yes. To live? *No.* Although I often think it might be nice to live without the constant barrage of messages on our cell phones. Or is it just mine that's constantly pinging at me?"

"It's not just yours."

He'd caught himself glancing at the screen of his phone more than once this morning, although he wasn't expecting to receive messages from anyone in particular. It was a habit. And not a good one. Holding Lea's hand, though, took care of that. Not to mention taking care of him being aware of anything except the feel of her skin against his.

"Where to next?"

Lea stood next to a wall that blocked the majority of the wind. She tugged her hand from his and readjusted the strings of her hat, tipping it off her head so that it hung down her back. Her dark locks gleamed in the light.

"There—I think that might be easier, actually."

He'd kind of liked her in the hat. Then again, he liked her with it off too. Their hands found each other once again, fingers linking this time.

"We can head up the hill toward some of the more impressive ruins. There's the amphitheater and Apollo's temple."

"Have they restored any of the ruins or are they just left natural?"

"They've restored some of them, but not all. The four remaining statues on the Terrace of the Lions are replicas. The originals are in the museum. We can see them on our way out."

They started walking, the easy camaraderie they'd suddenly developed making his defensiveness on Naxos fade away. Leaving it behind was hard. Because if there was one thing he knew how to do well it was defending his emotions from anything that might get too close.

Lea was definitely stepping nearer, and it had nothing to do with their holding hands.

Not that it made him let go. Or made him stop their arms from swinging back and forth in time as they walked up the narrow curving path. The warm, stiff breeze was now at their backs as they hiked up the hill toward the first of the ruins. The higher they went, the closer he had to lean to be heard over the wind.

He'd been to Delos many times, so he could almost recite the spiel of the tour guides by heart, but he knew that probably wasn't what Lea wanted to hear. And it wasn't what he wanted to say. He wanted to talk about the magic of the island. About the refuge he'd found here as a young adult, still struggling with the effects of his injuries.

But he didn't say any of that.

They came to the Terrace of the Lions and Lea's fascination was evident as she strained her neck to see the top. These statues—each perched on a stone rectangle—had seemed much larger when he was a child, but in reality, standing next to them, he saw that Lea's head reached the nearest lion's chest.

"I can't believe these aren't the originals."

The stone work was very good, and unless you were an expert in sculpting you'd probably never guess.

On impulse, Deakin took out his phone and snapped a picture of her. With her face tilted up, the wind catching the darks strands of her hair and sending them whipping around her face, she looked as if she belonged there. The urge to put his arm around her waist and haul her against him had been toying with his mind for several minutes. Maybe that was part of what was behind his sudden interest in photography. Anything to keep from scratching that other, more dangerous itch.

He could always send the shot to her as a keepsake of her day on the island. And then he would promptly delete it from his phone. He wasn't in the market for a wife, or even a girlfriend, but he could certainly appreciate a beautiful woman when he saw one.

And be affected by her. As evidenced on several occasions. Like now…

"What's next?" she asked, coming to stand beside him.

There was that itch again. Getting stronger all the time.

Stuffing the phone back in his pocket, he didn't even need to consult his map. "The sacred lake is just over there."

She turned her head and scanned the terrain in the direction he indicated. "Just over where?"

"There's no water in it anymore—it's been drained."

The natural bowl formed at the bottom of a depression was now dry.

"By the ancients?" Her voice had a breathless tone that he liked.

Hell, what *didn't* he like about her?

"No, it was done in the early twentieth century. There was an outbreak of malaria, and to prevent that from happening again they keep it empty."

"Wow—the sacred lake, done in by a bout of malaria." A choked laugh came out. "I know it's not funny, but…"

"It is—kind of." His fingers touched her waistline at the back of her dress. It was damp with perspiration. "Are you hot?"

"A little."

Deakin dropped his backpack to the ground and crouched beside it, taking out two bottles of water, both still very cold after having been stored in the boat's small freezer compartment. "We need to make sure we keep hydrated."

"Thanks." Twisting the top off, she tilted the bottle to her lips, seeming to caress the rim before tipping her head slightly as she took several long drinks.

From his position on the ground he could see the cords in her neck work as she swallowed. Her tongue then took a quick swipe at a drop of water that had escaped the bottle's opening and started down the side. He almost groaned aloud.

You need to curb that sick imagination of yours, bud.

He gulped some water himself, trying to wash down this unwelcome awareness of her that was steadily getting larger and harder to ignore. A certain part of his body was having the same problem.

He stood up to derail his thoughts. "Let's walk toward the museum. It's just across the way."

Lea screwed the cap back onto her water bottle. He held his hand out for it but she shook her head, holding the chilled bottle to the underside of her throat and closing her eyes.

"I think I'm going to hold onto this for a while. Besides, I know you have more stuff in there. Unless you'll let me carry it for a while?"

"I'm good. Seriously."

And the weight of the pack gave him something to think about. Anything to keep his mind off the way she was touching that bottle against different parts of her neck and sighing. Or the way her dress kept riding up those tanned thighs, despite her best efforts to keep everything battened down and secure.

His phone might not be taking snapshots anymore, but his brain certainly was. And these weren't the kind that could be deleted at the touch of a button.

They made their way past the Agora of the Italians and hiked along the Roman Wall. When they got to the Altar of Dionysus they stopped. Lea looked up at one of the two statues flanking the flat platform, her head tilted sideways as if trying to figure out exactly what…

She got it. And he had to smile. The two phallus monuments were kind of hard to miss.

"They are rather well endowed, aren't they?" she asked, laughter in her voice. "Or is that just wishful thinking?"

"Probably a little of both."

He'd had a few problems with his own…er… monument over the last half-hour or so. If she licked that water bottle one more time he was going to come unglued.

"It gives the idea of *'erecting'* a statue a whole new meaning." This time she giggled out loud.

"Yes, it does."

They finally made it to the museum, and stepped into the first shady area they'd seen on the island. There they found the four original lion statues, along with the Hand of Colossus and numerous other artifacts.

"This is better than some of the places on the mainland that I've visited. There is just so much history packed into such a tiny space."

"I think so too."

The skirt of her dress had been released and was on its best behavior now that the wind wasn't burrowing under it and teasing it away from her legs. *Damn.* Because he was thinking of doing that very thing himself…

Lea turned to look at something and bumped hard against Deakin's side in the process. "Sorry!"

His arm wrapped around her back to steady both of them, and that finally scratched the itch that had been plaguing him ever since they'd dropped anchor offshore. And, hell, if it didn't feel good…

Too good.

Soft green eyes came up to meet his. Her body was still pressed against him.

"Not your fault."

He tried to command his arm to drop back to his side, but since she was making no effort to pull away it was a hard sell. Especially since his own "Dionysus" was showing a whole lot of interest in keeping her right where she was…in the way she felt cradled against his body.

"I practically knocked you over."

"Not a chance."

Was it his imagination or had she turned to

face him slightly, her body fitting against his in a way that robbed his lungs of air?

He couldn't stop his arm from tightening its grip. His body was hyper-aware of every curve and dip of hers. It had been a long time since he'd felt this rush of need, and he was in no hurry to call an end to it. In fact…

His hands moved to cup her face, tilting it up slightly just as a slight movement to his right caught his eye.

Ignore it.

"Deakin?" she whispered.

He hovered, caught between two worlds. The one he wanted to be in—where pink parted lips were waiting—and the one that was slowly tugging at the duty center of his brain.

He allowed his glance to stray for just a second and spied a man leaning against one of the walls, right next to an exhibit of some marble busts. Hands on his knees, he appeared to be trying to catch his breath. No one seemed overly concerned, not even the man himself, but something was off.

He scanned the people near him, but either he was alone, or the person or group he was with was looking at something other than the man. His eyes came up at that moment and met Deakin's from across the room, and then his head dropped once again, his fingers gripping his legs more tightly.

Deakin swallowed, then looked back down at Lea. "Wait here for a minute," he murmured, before releasing her and making his way over to the man.

If there was nothing wrong with him Deakin was going to be kicking himself into next Tuesday.

The man was a little thick around the middle, and it could be that he was just out of shape and out of breath, but it wouldn't hurt to make sure.

He reached his side and put a hand on his shoulder. "Are you okay?"

"Can't…c-catch my breath." He paused in an attempt to draw in another wheezy puff of air.

"I'm a doctor. Mind if I check you—?"

At that moment the man's hands came off his knees and he crumpled right where he was, winding up in a sitting position, legs curled, head lolling to the left.

Lea was beside Deakin in an instant, dropping her water bottle and helping him lie the man out flat.

A crowd began forming around them, and he called out to the group. "Anyone know who he's with?"

Deakin's voice carried over the surrounding voices and someone stepped forward.

"I was on the same tour boat as he was, but I think he was alone. He didn't really speak to anyone that I saw. He caught my attention because of his backpack. It's from the same uni that I went to. Is he okay?"

"I don't know yet."

Deakin felt for a pulse and found one. It was quicker than it should be, and the man's skin was hot and dry. Not good at all.

He murmured to Lea. "I need your water bottle, if it's still cold."

"Here."

She pushed it into his hands and he thanked his lucky stars that he'd put them in the freezer on the boat before they'd left Mythelios. He placed the bottle against the man's neck, right where his carotid ran, hoping to cool the blood rushing through his system. He heard the zipper on his own backpack opening and soon three more bottles appeared, to be placed under the man's arms and on his groin—all blood-rich areas.

A tour guide came up and asked if she could help. Deakin quickly explained that he was a doctor and he thought the man might be suffering from heatstroke, and that they needed to get him cooled down as quickly as possible.

"I need to get him back to my boat and take him to hospital. It's air-conditioned."

The tour guide gathered some people who helped form a kind of mobile stretcher by linking hands beneath the man's body and lifting him.

"I don't know if this will work on some of those narrow areas, but if we can just crowd in close…"

They had to try. If the man was suffering from heatstroke he could very well die, since the part of his brain that regulated body temperature was shorting out.

It took fifteen minutes, but in Deakin's head it seemed like forever. He and Lea joined the rest of the group, grasping hands under the victim's legs and doing the best they could to synchronize their steps with those of the other rescuers. They would go through the man's pack as soon as they got to the boat and see if there was anything inside such as a medical alert bracelet, or an identity card listing any medication he might be taking.

Once they had him on board the boat, inside the main compartment on a small cushioned sofa, Lea thanked everyone. Then, with Deakin's help, she switched the air-conditioning on high while he started the boat.

"Can you try to get him cooled down while I drive?" he asked.

"Of course." She had already opened one of the water bottles and was dousing the man with it. "I'll get some of his clothes off and keep using the water."

Deakin aimed one of the air-conditioning vents so it pointed directly at the patient. "There are more bottles in the freezer. And there's potable water in the tank that runs the taps."

"Go. I've got this."

Deakin went up to the wheelhouse and started the engines, while some of the folks who'd helped them untied the ropes from the cleats on the dock and tossed them onto the vessel.

"Thanks!" he yelled above the engines.

Time to get this man to the nearest capable facility—which was probably their clinic on Mythelios.

For once he felt a sense of urgency rather than dread as he prepared to go back to the island. He gunned the engine and hoped that Lea had everything secured down below as he backed out of the slip on the dock and shoved the gear lever into drive. Then he throttled up, kicking a spray of foam to the side as he spun the boat and headed back the way they'd came.

They'd be bypassing Naxos, though. There was just something in him telling him that Mythelios was the best place for this man to be.

He picked up his radio and called the deck below. He flicked the switch that would allow him to hear what was being said down there, then depressed the call button.

"Lea, what's happening?"

"You can hear me?"

Of course. She had no idea there were speakers downstairs that would pick up her voice. His dad had installed them on the original *Mytheliostocracy* to keep in contact with his mother during trips. And he'd had a duplicate system put on the *Mytheliostocracy II*.

"Yes. There are microphones set up in the speakers. How's he doing?"

"He's still unconscious, but I think cooling him off is working. His pulse isn't quite as thready as it was. Your air-conditioning works great. Too bad the clinic doesn't have its own boat. It could go out on rescues just like this one."

He blinked. They had boats bringing in patients from time to time, but they'd never really discussed having a vessel of their own.

"We're about twenty-five minutes out— maybe a little less if I can coax some more power from this engine."

"I think the important thing is that we arrive in one piece."

A ghost of a smile played around the edges of his mind. "Worried?"

"About the patient. Not about me."

"I'm being as safe as I can."

Which was true. He didn't take as many risks as he had when he was younger. Maybe that made him a boring person. But at least he didn't put anyone else in danger. When he thought about what could have happened to his parents' house, and to them, if that explosion had been any bigger...

Come on, Deakin. Let's just worry about someone you can help.

"I'll keep the intercom on. Let me know if you need anything. I'm going to call ahead to the clinic and tell Petra to be ready with an ice bath."

"Good idea."

He let Lea get back to working on the patient, and realized as he did so that he had no problem turning the man's care over to her—something that was unusual for him. He was used to being given free rein with his patients, since burn specialists were not a dime a dozen. But this wasn't a burn patient—and, more than that, he trusted her. It was as simple as that. He'd already seen how fiercely she cared about her own patients—it was part of the reason for their little verbal scuffle over on Naxos. She would do her very best for their heatstroke victim.

As soon as he'd alerted Petra, who said they'd be ready when they got there, he put the receiver back up to his mouth to talk to Lea.

"I know we didn't find any kind of medical alert items, but can you go through his backpack again and look for some kind of contact information?"

"Already done. His name is Sam Davidson. He's an American. I only found his mother's name and phone number, so I called and left a voicemail. Hopefully she'll get in contact with me soon."

"Good work. We're getting close. About ten minutes out, I think."

"Sounds good."

He heard her talking to their patient in low, calm tones, asking him to open his eyes if he could hear her. Impatience rose inside him. He wanted to be down there helping, dammit. Not stuck up here driving the boat. He couldn't see how EMT drivers did it.

"He's waking up." Lea's voice came through, then the sound of thrashing and a man's loud voice. "He's a little miffed, I think."

Her voice changed, turning into the bossy Lea he'd met a time or two.

"No, wait. You can't… You need to…"

Then…

"Deakin, we may have a problem down here."

Just then he heard a crash and the sound of glass breaking somewhere below.

"Lea? What's going on? Hey! Answer me!"

A few seconds later, she did. "It's okay. He's just confused. He's lying down again now."

Relief swamped his system. "Do you need me to stop the boat and come down there?"

"No. He broke a drinking glass, that's all. He's fine."

A man's voice came, sounding shaky and weak. "Sorry to be a problem."

"Hey, it's no problem. We're headed to a clinic on our island. They can help with whatever's going on."

"Thank you."

Deakin should be the one thanking *him*. While he certainly hadn't wanted anyone to get sick, their patient had succeeded in doing what all the mental gymnastics in the world hadn't been able to do: taking his mind off his own base desires and putting it on something that might actually do some good.

CHAPTER SEVEN

"YOU'RE GOING TO be fine."

Sam Davidson had spent a few days at the clinic before getting the green light to go home. Heatstroke could cause multiple organ failure, but this particular patient had dodged that bullet. Maybe it was because they'd been able to get those water bottles on him so quickly. Or maybe it was pure luck. Whatever it was, Lea was glad.

Watching Deakin take his vitals at the museum had made something shift in her tummy. She'd been so focused on what she'd hoped was about to happen between them that she'd totally tuned out everything else around them. Until Deakin had told her to wait and quickly headed toward the stranger.

His tan had darkened further since he'd been on the island, making his scars stand out. Those areas had lost all their melanin, either during the healing process or during some of the grafting procedures he'd undergone. But she'd seen them enough now that they just seemed part of what made him Deakin—even though still she wasn't entirely sure who that was.

Just when she thought she was getting to know him, he fooled her and became someone else completely. And that scared her. She wasn't sure why. She wasn't engaged to this man, like she'd been to Mark. What he wanted to do with his life should be of no importance to her.

And it wasn't.

At least she hoped it wasn't.

"How long before I can catch a flight home?"

Their patient's voice called her from her thoughts.

Their patient. Theirs. As in his and hers.

Um, *no*. She was not going to start thinking in those terms.

"Well, if you lived on the mainland we would have already discharged you. But flights from here to the States aren't the shortest. I just want to wait another day or so. Surely our food isn't all that bad?"

"Actually, it's pretty good. I just know my mom is worried and would like me home."

"It won't be much longer," Deakin said with a smile.

Sam lay back against the pillows and glanced at Deakin. "You saved my life."

"No. There were a lot of people who helped—including those who carried you from the museum to the boat."

"I know. I wish I could thank them all."

"We've had a couple of people call and ask about you. Unfortunately our laws are similar to your HIPPA rules. We couldn't say much. Maybe once you leave you'll give us permission to let them know you're okay."

"Of course I will. I'll sign whatever you need."

"Great—thank you."

Petra stuck her head into the room. "Theo wants to see you for a minute."

"Who? Me?" Lea wasn't sure why he would want to talk to *her*.

"No, Deakin."

Her voice sounded a little bit ominous.

Deakin must be thinking the exact same thing, because a vein had begun pulsing in his temple.

"I'll be out in a minute. Thanks." He turned back to his patient. "I'll be back sometime this afternoon to check on you again. Hopefully I'll have a better idea of when you can get out of this place."

"Thanks again for all you did. I am very grateful."

"Just be careful out in the heat for a while. There's some evidence that heatstroke can permanently alter your ability to regulate your temperature. So make sure you see your own doctors once you get home. They'll be able to tell you the best way to proceed."

"Why did it even happen? I'm from Florida. It gets plenty hot there."

"Greece has a dryer climate than Florida. You can dehydrate without realizing it." He patted the man on the shoulder. "But it looks like you're on the mend. Just monitor your water intake and make sure you're getting enough even if you don't feel thirsty."

"I definitely will after this." Sam's glance moved to include her. "Thank you both."

Lea smiled at him. "We're just glad you're going to be okay."

"So am I."

Deakin moved to the door and opened it. "Get some rest while you can. I'm sure once you're home you're not going to have much time for that."

They'd discovered, after he'd opened up to Lea one day, that Sam was a stockbroker—it was a job, he said, that ran him ragged. He'd come to Greece hoping to get out of the rat race for a little while. Instead he'd landed himself in the hospital.

Following Deakin out, she wondered what Theo wanted with him. Hopefully Cailey was okay…

And there he was. Waiting for Deakin by the reception desk.

"What do you need, Theo?" he asked.

The other doctor glanced at her for a moment and she backed away. "I think I have a patient coming in a few minutes, so I'm going to run. See you later."

Without looking behind her she turned and hightailed it out of there.

Before she got dragged into whatever was about to go down between the two men.

"All right, Theo, she's gone. Now, spit it out."

It was obvious his friend hadn't wanted to say whatever it was he wanted to say in front of the psychiatrist.

"How do you like working with her?"

His brain went on high alert. Had Theo sensed something unprofessional in his demeanor toward Lea? There had certainly been a few moments on the island when he'd almost stepped over the line of professionalism. But no one knew that except for Lea and him…

"She seems to be good at her job. Patients like her. What is this all about?"

Had he found something bad on her record?

"Do you think she's been valuable to the clinic?"

There was something about the way Theo was asking these questions that made him suspicious. "In as far as her work ethic goes? Or are you talking about her profession itself?"

"Either. Both. Is there something you don't like about her?"

That was the problem. He pretty much liked *everything* about her. Well, her profession itself made him a little uncomfortable, but that wasn't her problem—it was his.

"No. I think she's done a great job—especially since she's a *volunteer.*" Maybe now was the time to bring up the subject of payment.

Theo regarded him for a second. "And if she weren't?"

"Are you thinking of paying her? Because my answer would be that it's about damn time."

"Okay. It's settled, then. I want to call a meeting of the board of directors to make it official. I can at least get Chris online and ask for his input, and I can make another attempt to contact Ares. The clinic is short of funds after the earthquake, but I feel like she's worked hard and has more than earned any proposed income."

"Sounds good. Let me know when the others can meet and I'll clear my schedule."

Theo smiled. "Sounds good. I was afraid you were going to put the kibosh on the suggestion."

"No kiboshing going on here. Do you want me to let her know?"

Great, now he was looking for excuses to talk to her?

"No, I'd like to do it myself, if you don't mind."

"I'm okay with that." Deakin paused. "How's Stavros, by the way? Have you heard anything?"

"Not a peep out of him. I think I may have to pay him a visit…unless maybe *you* want to."

"Ha! Last time we almost ended up punching each other out. It's time for me to say, *Tag, you're it.*"

"Thanks, bud. You never did have much of a bedside manner."

"I never needed one."

"You are a regular riot, Deak."

He laughed. "I do my best." He sobered a bit. "And Cailey? She's still okay?"

His friend's face softened. "She's great. *We're* great."

"I'm happy for you. I really am."

When he'd first heard that Theo had found someone the news had shaken him. It had made his own aloneness feel that little bit sharper. But now that he'd had time to think about it he could congratulate Theo without feeling the world was coming to an end.

"Thanks. That means a lot. I hope Chris and Ares are as happy with their lives—wherever they are."

"Me too. I'm headed out to lunch. If you need something, give me a yell."

"I will."

Deakin decided to stop by the reception desk and see if there were any patients who hadn't been seen and then go grab something to eat himself.

He wasn't exactly sure what else he could help with on the island now the earthquake repairs were well underway. But, like Lea, he was between assignments, so he might as well stick around for a few more weeks before contacting the relief organization and seeing where they could use him next.

Or maybe he really should start looking for something a little more permanent.

Here on the island?

Hell, no. He'd never feel all warm and cuddly about Mythelios—at least he didn't think he would. When he was here all he could think about was how soon he could leave again. With the exception of his aunt, Stavros, and his buddies at the clinic, there was no one he really cared about here on the island. Oh, he would die trying to save any one of the islanders, but he would do that wherever he was.

Petra was seated behind the glassed-in desk, talking to a patient. He waited for her to finish and then went up to her. "Who's next?"

"Hello, Dr. Patera. How *are* you?"

The sardonic drawl was unmistakable. Maybe he *was* a little short with people at times. He held up his hands. "Okay, I'm—"

"Don't tell me the inestimable Dr. Deakin Patera is about to *apologize*." She put her hand over her heart as if having palpitations.

He laughed. "I was going to, but now…"

"Apology accepted."

"I don't remember actually getting that far, but okay."

His gaze went to the wall beside her, noticing immediately the empty nail where the calendar had been. July had hit several days earlier, and he'd been meaning to come over and ask her to take it down. Maybe someone else had gotten to it first, or perhaps Theo had had mercy on him and done as he'd asked. Whatever it was, he was grateful.

"Anything else?" she asked.

"Yes. Thanks for taking that down."

"What down?"

He nodded at the wall.

She looked beside her and her eyes widened. "I didn't do that. But don't worry…" She reached down and opened a drawer and pulled out another calendar. "I have plenty more where that came from."

He groaned. "Can't you just leave it down?"

"Not if I want to eat."

"Sorry?"

"We're running on fumes right now at the clinic, so this calendar has been bringing in quite a bit of money. Having one hanging there is great advertising for it."

When she flipped it open to July he couldn't stand it. "I'm out of here. Unless there are more patients that need to be seen."

"I think Lea took the last one on the list to the Serenity Gardens."

So she hadn't just been making an empty excuse about having a patient a little earlier.

"Okay. Call me if Sam's condition changes." In case she didn't know who he meant, he added, "The heatstroke patient."

"Are you headed home or to lunch?"

He glanced at his watch. Just two-thirty. Theo had said he was headed to lunch, but he hadn't thought to ask if his friend was coming back afterwards or not.

Maybe he should just go grab something from the clinic's little café. Or maybe he should head to Stavros's place to get something to eat and a little something else to drown his sorrows—the sorrows that came from almost kissing your work colleague. But drinking alcohol this early…? Probably not the best idea. Especially if he had to see patients afterwards.

Well, lunch it was. At the small cafeteria. And then he would finish his day, go home, and forget about a certain island and a certain woman and the fact that he'd had fun for the first time in a very long time. And he'd also do his best to forget that she currently lived less than twenty steps away from where he slept.

The smoke alarm went off at exactly nine p.m., its shrill whistle firing up his nervous system like a lightning bolt. He shot up from the sofa, yanking his T-shirt on over his head and grabbing his shoes, then careened through the door and across the lawn.

It wasn't coming from the main house. It was the cottage again. As fast as it had started, it stopped. He stood there in the grass for a moment, waiting. Maybe she'd just burned her eggs again. After all, he'd shown her how to work the remote control to turn the alarm off if it was a false alarm.

Did he go back inside, or did he go over there and make sure things were okay? What if there was a fire and she was trying to deal with it on her own?

The siren blared again, lasting a few seconds longer this time before cutting out. That made his decision. Not bothering to put his shoes on, he finished jogging across the space before banging on the front door. She opened it almost immediately, not saying a word, just spinning around and walking back inside, moving toward the dining room.

He didn't smell smoke. Or see any evidence of it. She turned toward him, picked up the remote and hit a button. Like clockwork, the alarm went off again. This time he went over and took it out of her hand and shut the thing off.

"What the hell, Lea? I don't know what you think you're doing, but this isn't funny. Nor is it a game." His blood pressure had spiked sky-high, and his chest was tight with a familiar stinging fear.

"Do I *look* like I'm playing a game?"

He peered down at her and realized that, while he might have broken out in a cold sweat,

Lea was trembling—but not with fear. With anger.

"I don't understand, but if you ever set that off again…"

"You'll what?"

"I'll have to ask you to leave."

Her chin went up. "Then go ahead. Ask."

He was at a loss. Surely she hadn't just set it off to torment him? She didn't even know what had led him to have the system installed.

"Please don't turn it on again."

"Fine. I won't. If you'll do *me* the favor of—" She picked something up off the bar in the kitchen and walked over to where he was standing. She slammed it on the table. "Telling me what the meaning of *this* is."

His eyes tracked to the item. And he groaned. It was the stupid calendar, and it was opened to *his* page.

"Where did you get that?"

"Off the wall in the reception area."

So that was where it had gone. "It's just a fundraiser. I wasn't even supposed to be in it. Someone was sick and I had to fill in."

"That doesn't answer my question." Her mouth was tight with anger. "What is *this*?"

"Listen, I know I don't measure up to the rest of the men in it, but it was either that or scrap the project—"

"Don't measure up? I'm not talking about that, dammit. I'm talking about *this*!" She pushed it closer.

His eyes flicked to the image and then away. It was him without his shirt on. Big deal. Had she tricked him into coming over here to try to humiliate him?

"Tear it out if you don't like it. I don't give a damn."

"God, Deakin. You are dense. *Look* at it."

"No. Just tell me what's wrong with it so I can go home."

"It's been altered. You had all your scars removed. Why?"

What? He allowed his gaze to go back to the picture and forced himself to look at it this time. She was right. The left side of his face, neck and chest were as clean and clear as the right side of his body. The scars had been whisked away. This was what he would have looked like if the accident had never happened.

He didn't blame the calendar company. *He* didn't like looking at the damage to his body, so why would anyone else?

"Maybe the photographer actually wanted to *sell* some calendars."

"You…" Her nose scrunched up as if trying to contain whatever it was she wanted to say.

"Are you saying you didn't *ask* them to remove your scars during the touch up phase?"

"I didn't. But I'm relieved they did."

He hadn't even looked at the photo until now. It was kind of fascinating to see himself without those scars. Without the consequences of a stupid teenaged decision that had changed his life forever.

"They're a part of who you are. They don't look as bad as you probably think they do."

This time it was his turn to get mad. She had no idea what she was talking about. Where did she get off, saying something like that? And to set off that alarm just to force him to come over so she could tell him off... *Not happening.*

"Oh, they're plenty bad, lady."

"Show me."

"Like hell."

He didn't go anywhere without his shirt on. Except to get his damn picture taken for all the world to see, evidently. And even that didn't get him a free pass.

She slung the calendar off the table, letting it hit the ground with a thud. "That's not who you really are."

"Maybe it's who I *wish* I was."

She was mad at him over a stupid picture? Well, he'd see if he could make her even angrier.

"Okay, fine. You're so good at psychoanalyzing people? Analyze *this*!"

His hot breath sawing in and out of his lungs, he reached down and gripped the bottom of his T-shirt, then tore it up and over his head, letting it drop to the ground.

He didn't look down at himself. He already knew exactly what he looked like. Lea did, though, sliding her gaze over his chest, her brows furrowing as she studied him.

All the anger seemed to drop out of her in an instant. Just as he'd suspected. She was shocked. Horrified. Ready to beg him to put his clothes back on.

She didn't. Instead she went and picked up the calendar and opened it to his picture. She looked closely at it. Then at the true image. This time she didn't fling it away from her. She set it carefully down on the table.

"That picture isn't you, Deakin. And if you think the real you disgusts me, you're wrong." Her voice lowered to a whisper. "Oh, *so* wrong."

He swallowed hard. It almost sounded as if she…

He wasn't sure if she moved first or if he did, but they were suddenly gripping each other with desperate hands, his mouth slamming on top of hers with a fervency he'd never felt before. She didn't try to tug free, or even hesitate. Her lips opened wide, her hands going to the back of his head and pulling him closer.

Hell. He groaned, his tongue surging into the vacuum and tasting coffee and her own sweet essence. He'd wanted to kiss her back on Delos, and would have if not for Sam and his heatstroke. But all that was now washed away under a tsunami of need.

Her fingers left his head and trailed down the side of his neck, following something. His scars. Only this time it didn't make him want to jerk away. It made him want to lose himself inside her, to let her touch him and do whatever she wanted.

He frowned slightly when she reached the part of his chest wall that was devoid of sensation. From his shoulder to just below his nipple his skin was completely numb. He fought the urge to stop her, to take her hand and place it where he *could* feel it—feel *her*.

Except this was what she wanted to do. This was what their conversation had been leading up to. Or maybe it had been headed here since that moment in the reception area when she'd mistaken him for a patient. The attraction had certainly been there on his part. And evidently on hers too.

His hands came up and wrapped around her

upper arms before sliding up and cupping her face, just the way he had on Delos. Her skin was as soft as he remembered, making him want to do all kinds of things to her.

And she wanted to do things to him too. Easing her head back, she looked up at him, fingers still tracing over his ruined flesh.

"These are part of who you are. And you are very, *very* sexy. Therefore, according to every algebra problem I've ever solved, that must mean these are sexy too."

God, he wanted her. Right now. Before he had a chance to think or reason…or regret.

He scooped her up and carried her down the tiny hallway to where he knew the bedroom was. If she wanted to stop him, she would. He knew by now that she was not afraid of confrontation. Of saying what she thought needed to be said.

She didn't say anything, though. She simply wrapped her arms around his neck and leaned her face against his chest, nuzzling the underside of his chin. His need ratcheted up even higher.

He reached the bedroom and nudged open the door with his bare foot, his soles sinking into the deep carpet of the rug inside. He could lay her right on that floor and be happy. But there was also the bed. And he would be even happier there.

Tossing her onto the silk coverlet, he took the time to look at the way she was splayed out, all soft and sexy, her eyes filled with anticipation.

Bending over her, he planted his palms on either side of her face and leaned in for a kiss. "If you aren't wanting this to go any further, say it now."

"I *am* wanting this to go further. *Much* further."

She linked her hands behind his neck and tugged his face down, urging him to kiss her once again. He was more than happy to oblige. When his chest brushed her breasts the contrast between soft and hard arrowed straight to his groin. He groaned.

Then she was touching him again, stroking places that were numb and places that were not. He pressed a knee between her legs, relishing the way she gripped it between her thighs. Soon she'd be gripping something else…

Suddenly palms went to his chest and she was pushing. He was up and off her in an instant.

"No, no. It's okay."

She came up on her knees, reaching for his hands and pulling him forward again. This time when she shifted him he realized what she wanted and it made parts of him jerk. She twisted until she had maneuvered him onto the bed, flat on his back, with her straddling his hips. Her palms skated down his chest, and when she leaned over and took his left nipple in her mouth he shuddered.

He couldn't feel it, but he could damned well imagine it. And it made other senses come alive. He could still experience the thrill of having her lips on him. The tiny suckling sounds she made, the scent of her hair so close to his nose. The heat of her body on the rest of him.

Then she moved over to the other nipple and his hips surged forward, almost lifting off the bed. Okay, he could feel that, and it was... *electrifying*.

Her pelvis found his erection and ground hard against it.

"Hell..."

If she kept that up, he was a goner.

He gripped her hips, holding them still for several long seconds. It didn't help. They might have stopped moving but her lips certainly hadn't, grazing over the side of his jaw, biting at the joint of his neck.

Like lightning, he flipped her back over. "My turn, honey."

Only he didn't kiss her. He reached for the lightweight knit top she had on and hauled it over her head. He'd half hoped she wouldn't have a bra on, but at least it had a front clasp. He saw the little joiner thing right between those luscious breasts.

He slid a finger beneath it and popped it open before peeling apart the cups, revealing tight puckered nipples. But there was no time to kiss them. Not yet. He wanted her clothes off. All of them. *Then* he would let himself explore.

Climbing off the bed, he noted that her eyes weren't shut. They were watching every move he made, their green irises burning with an inner heat that made him ache.

Off came her bottoms—stretchy exercise pants—gliding over her hips and down her long legs with ease. Legs that would soon be wrapped around his hips as he thrust home.

He swallowed. Things were moving too fast, and yet he was powerless to slow them down. "Promise me we'll do this again."

She didn't ask him what he meant. "I promise."

Taking his wallet from his pants, he flipped it open, hoping against hope that he had something.

Before he could look, she took it from him

and tossed it aside. "I'm protected. And clean. And I want to *feel* you."

Damn. She made even condom talk sexy.

He didn't argue—just unzipped his jeans as Lea sat up to watch. That made him hot. The way her attention was fully on what was happening in front of her.

His jeans and briefs went down, and then he was free. Her hands immediately went to the backs of his thighs, just below his ass, and tugged him forward, her tongue moistening her lips in preparation.

"No. That comes the next time. Because first I want…*this*."

He bore her back onto the bed, shuddering with need when she parted her legs and hooked her feet around the back of his calves. He wanted her. Desperately. But he needed to do something first.

Still standing, and with the high bed providing the perfect height, he used his aching flesh to trace along her skin from her knees to her thighs. Her low moan revved him up in a way nothing else could. Over and over he brushed himself along her skin, the sensation taking him almost to breaking point. Then he moved forward to the place where the space narrowed to one tiny point between her legs. He touched the juncture. Then repeated the gesture. Her gasp told him he was in just the right spot.

Planting her feet on the edge of the bed, she lifted slightly so that she could press against him in rhythmic bursts. Her eyes fluttered closed as she continued to pleasure herself. Then she brushed his hand aside and gripped him, her fingers tight and needy as she did the job herself, pumping along him, teeth burrowing into her lower lip in the way that he loved.

And then she was over the edge, her sharp cry tearing through him. He lined himself up in a hurry and thrust home. *Hard.* The squeeze of her body took his senses and focused them into a blurred jumble of heat, wet, and sweet, tight friction. He wasn't going to last. Didn't want to last. She'd promised him more and he was going to take her at her word.

Gripping her ass, he thrust again and again, leaning in and taking her moans into his mouth. Then he finally let himself go, felt a sharp burst of pleasure ripping through him and slashing his world in two. In three. In four. Until it was in tiny pieces that he wasn't sure could ever be put back together.

Satiation snuck in, taking the edge off the furious pace, and his movements slowed, became languorous.

And then he was done, finally allowing

himself to press his body fully against hers. She was damp with perspiration, her lids still squeezed tightly together.

A tiny fragment of worry penetrated the bliss.

Open your eyes, Lea.

Was she afraid to look at him? Maybe all that talk about his scars being a part of who he was had been just that. Talk.

No, she'd been genuinely angry at him when she'd thought *he'd* had those scars on the calendar altered. So it wasn't that she was horrified by them. At least she hadn't been a few minutes ago.

Hadn't she said they were sexy? No. She'd said *he* was sexy.

Wasn't it the same thing?

Right now, he wasn't sure of anything.

He found his voice and used it. "Hey. Are you okay?"

"Mmm…" Green eyes appeared, poring over his face. "Just trying to gear myself up to keep a certain promise."

Relief washed over him and he gathered her in his arms, turning her so they were facing each other. "Regretting that promise already?"

"Oh, no. Not at all."

"That's good—because neither am I. In fact

as soon as I catch my breath I think I'll be ready for the second course."

"Second?" Her lips curved. "How many courses *are* there in this particular feast?"

"I would say it's open-ended. There can be as few or as many as we want."

Her fingertips came up and brushed over his temples. "In that case, if you don't mind, I plan on being very, *very* greedy."

Anticipation trickled through him, causing a chain reaction that began to spread its tentacles along him.

"Oh, Lea. I was so hoping you'd say that…"

CHAPTER EIGHT

HE'D MADE HER forget about Mark. At least for a night. As she sat in her little floral alcove in the clinic's garden and tried to concentrate on what her patient was saying she was still thrilled. And terrified.

She'd been so sure he'd asked to have those scars covered up in that picture, so he could pretend they had never happened. But he hadn't. It had been some stupid photographer instead.

But she didn't regret confronting him. It had paid off in spades. He'd made love to her multiple times in multiple positions, each more exciting and different than the last. And when they'd parted ways this morning it hadn't seemed as awkward as it might have. Although Deakin hadn't been particularly talkative. Then again, neither had she. She hadn't wanted to spoil what they'd shared together.

Blinking, she focused again on her patient

and put Deakin out of her mind once and for all. Not an easy task. But then she hadn't expected it to be.

She somehow made it through the session, even got some important things accomplished during it, and when she went out to the reception desk she found Theo there.

He motioned her over. "Can I talk to you for a second?"

Her heart stopped for a beat or two, before galloping off at the speed of light. Did he know about her and Deakin? Did she have some big goofy smile on her face or something? Oh, Lord, she hoped not. That would be mortifying.

Why? Hadn't he and Cailey found love in the aftermath of the earthquake?

That was different.

Um...how, exactly, Lea?

"Sure. Here?"

"It's nothing Petra hasn't already heard me say. I just needed to talk to Deakin before approaching you."

Trepidation moved over her. Oh, God, had Deakin told him about what they'd done together? Or, worse yet, maybe they'd decided they didn't need her anymore and were going to ask her to leave.

She didn't want to go to back to Canada.

Not yet, anyway. She wanted to stay here—even though she'd told herself time and time again that that wasn't going to be an option. Hadn't Deakin said last night that the calendars were a fundraising tool because of a shortfall in their budget? How exactly did she expect them to be able to pay another staff member when they already were having trouble supporting the ones they had?

"Okay… Is something wrong?"

"No. Not at all. In fact I think we're going to ask you to stay on here at the clinic. Is that a possibility?"

She went from thinking she was going to be fired to going to be hired. Was he serious?

She asked him as much. "I love it here. Are you telling me that I might be offered a permanent position?"

His answer was a smile.

Still not sure she was reading him correctly, she glanced at Petra, who was nodding vigorously. And smiling too. "Congratulations!"

"Wow, this isn't what I expected to hear today."

Theo leaned a shoulder against the wall. "Oh? What *were* you expecting?"

That was something she wasn't going to tell anyone. Especially not Theo or Petra.

"I'm not sure. You already discussed this with Deakin?"

"I already did. He was in favor of it."

That shocked her. He'd given no indication last night that he and Theo had talked about hiring her. Did that mean he *wanted* her to stay?

A thread of happiness uncoiled inside her before she could stop it. She hurried to wind it back, afraid this was all one big joke.

Would she be able to work with him without imagining him naked? Without remembering exactly what they'd done in bed? She wasn't sure, and that scared her the most.

"Can I think about it for a day or so and get back with you?"

"Of course. I thought this was something you'd maybe already considered, though."

"It's the chance of a lifetime, actually. I was looking to move on from… Well, to move on from my previous location. So I'm having a hard time believing this is actually happening."

"I can understand that. It's a big decision."

Huge. Gigantic. *Gargantuan.*

She would have leaped at the offer a few short weeks ago. But now…?

Actually, now she still wanted it. Deakin or no Deakin. Surely they could learn to work together in a professional way, leaving their private lives in the bedroom? Not that it was even certain they were going to do what they'd done last night again.

But the decision about whether to stay or go had to be separate from her decision about being with Deakin. If she tied them together, making one dependent on the other, then she would be doing herself a disservice. Especially when she didn't really understand what made the man tick. *Yet.*

She wanted to stay. That was the one certainty she kept circling around to.

"I think I've changed my mind. I'd like to go ahead and give you my decision now if I could."

"Of course." He moved his propped shoulder away from the wall as if going on high alert.

"If you're serious about the offer, I'd like to accept it."

"I am *very* serious. I've already called a meeting with the other partners just to make sure everyone is on board, but I'm sure it's just a formality. You've already proven yourself capable and the patients love you. Even the ones who aren't here specifically for counseling."

"I'm glad. I love the people on the island, as well."

He held out his hand and she squeezed it. "I'll get everyone together and get the details hammered out. I'm not yet sure what salary package we can offer you, though."

"As long as I can afford a place to live and food in my refrigerator I'll be fine."

"I'm sure we can find you a few more euros than that. You don't think you'll stay in Deakin's cottage? It's been a rental in the past. And he rarely sticks around for long."

That made her swallow hard. Was he even now getting ready to leave, after only a couple of weeks? Was that why he'd decided that making love with her was safe…because he was already on his way out?

Wouldn't that be easier, though, than having him stay? The second things went south with them she would be out and looking for a new place to work.

He'd only come because of the earthquake—he'd said that himself. And, actually, he had no great love for his home island that she could see. He'd seemed happy to be on Naxos, and even happier to be on Delos. Which was sad. She loved Toronto, despite Mark's death. But his suicide was what had caused her to want to move on to a new place. Maybe Deakin was the same. Because of the fire?

The scars on his chest were worse than she'd imagined, although she'd done her damnedest to make sure he didn't see her shock. The two big scars running down the side of his neck changed once they reached his torso. There the scars looked as if something had landed on his chest and exploded in place. The damage must have been extensive and destructive. No wonder he was so sensitive about it. She would be too.

When she'd touched him there she'd expected a violent reaction, but there hadn't been one. She suspected the nerve-endings in his skin had been adversely affected. And yet, he'd let her stay there and explore, hadn't tried to move her over to where it felt better…to a place he was more comfortable with.

A lump formed in her throat that she couldn't swallow away.

"I don't know what I'll do yet as far as where I'll live. I think that will depend on a lot of things. I expect some of the boarding houses will be opening up for clients shortly."

"I think you're right." He shoved his hands in his pockets. "Well, that's what I wanted to tell you. I'm surprised Petra hasn't jumped in before now to express her opinion." He gave the woman a quick grin that said he knew her well.

She didn't let him down. "That's because you already know what I think. All I can add is that it's about damned time. I've been waiting on you all to do something before we lose her to somewhere else."

Moisture pricked holes in the backs of Lea's eyelids. If she wanted to make a fresh start, far from the tragedy of her past, this was her chance. And she'd be a fool if she turned this opportunity down.

"Thank you. That means a lot, coming from you."

"Well, I'll let you go," said Theo. "I'll get back to you with the details once we have our meeting."

"Okay—thanks again for everything."

With that Theo turned and headed down the hallway toward his office.

She turned to Petra. "Are you sure they'll all want me to stay?"

"I'd say they'd better. Or they'll have me to contend with. And I think they know better than to get on my bad side."

Lea smiled. She had no doubt that Petra's bad side was a place no one wanted to land on. But from what Theo had said she wouldn't need Petra or anyone to plead her case. Asking her to stay was already a done deal. At least according to Theo it was.

Deakin was shoving a screwdriver into a stuck door-lock in one of the exam rooms when a pair of shoes came into view. Worn leather loafers were joined by a pair of faded jeans that had seen better days.

Deakin straightened and frowned when he realized it wasn't a stranger after all. Dark hair and an even darker beard shadowed a tanned face. A familiar face, but one that looked very different from the one he was used to seeing. There had been a time when charm and sophistication had been the cornerstones of this man's life. That charm was nowhere in evidence right now.

"Ares? Is that you?"

The green duffle bag perched on his shoulder was hefted around and dropped on the ground with a loud thud. Several people turned to stare. He was one of their own, but so far no one except Deakin had recognized him.

"Well, it's not my ghost. Not yet anyway."

Ares Xenakis had been part of their tight little circle growing up. Like Deakin and Chris, he had chosen to go through medical school and then get off the island. It looked as if the earthquake really was bringing them all trickling back in. After it was over they would stream back out. At least some of them would—Deakin being one of them.

"Some might argue with that. You look like

you've been through hell and come out the other side."

His friend laughed. "Not quite." His face went serious again. "I came as soon as I could."

"Me too." Deakin hadn't been all that polished when he'd arrived either, but Ares might very well have him beaten. "You look like you could use sixty hours of sleep."

"That feels about right. That cottage of yours open? I could go home, but I've been in the air or laid over for almost thirty straight hours straight. I'm dead on my feet."

Ares had his own residence on a tiny neighboring island, but Deakin could certainly understand being so tired that you could no longer put one foot in front of the other. He'd been there a time or two himself. The problem was his cottage wasn't vacant—and there was no way he was going to suggest Lea share it with Ares, no matter how innocent it might be. Especially since it only had one bedroom.

Why he suddenly felt that way he had no idea. Men were supposed to be able to have sex without it affecting them emotionally, right? Then why did he feel so damned...*affectionate* towards her? A word he had never in his life associated with his personality.

It had to be the time they'd spent together

on Delos. It had thrown them both for a loop. Or was it more than that?

"The cottage is rented out at the moment, but the apartment over the boathouse is empty. Or you can stay in one of the guest rooms at the main house."

"If that place is still the mausoleum it used to be, then I'll take the boathouse. With the state I'm in now, I'd probably leave three layers of dirt on everything I touched. Your aunt would have a fit."

"I doubt that. She's going to welcome you like a long-lost son."

Ares glanced around. "She'll be the only one, from the looks of it. My secret agent disguise is evidently working. At least for now. Maybe I'll keep this look for a while."

"Be prepared to be arrested for vagrancy, then."

"That bad?"

"I would say I've seen worse, but…"

"Funny."

Deakin gave Ares' shoulder a quick squeeze. "I'll call Theo and let him know you're here."

"There'll be plenty of time for reunions. Besides, I texted him last night and told him I was on my way. I'm surprised he didn't say anything to you."

There was no way Deakin was going to tell

his friend that he'd been too busy last night to have answered *any* call other than the call of the wild…

"Do you want me to take you to the house?"

"No, I've got it. I know where your key is too. That smoke alarm isn't going to go off on me, is it?"

He pointed his screwdriver at his friend's chest. "As long as you don't set anything on fire you'll be fine."

Deakin had already had the scare of his life last night from someone setting off that damned alarm. And then Lea had shocked the hell out of him. In more ways than one.

His teeth gritted when that "affectionate" gene poked its head out again and threatened to spread around some cute little endearments. He had to play whack-a-mole with it a few times before he was finally able to shove it down in its hidey-hole.

"I'll be back when I've had those sixty hours of sleep and feel like a human being again."

Deakin grinned. "In that case it might be a year or two before anyone realizes the island's prodigal has finally returned."

"I'd forgotten just how hilarious you are."

At that moment Lea chose to come around the corner. She froze when she saw Ares. But, since his face wasn't one of the ones on the calendar, she had no way of knowing who he was.

"Lea, I'd like you to meet Ares Xenakis. Ares, this is Dr. Lea Risi. Ares is an old friend of mine. And a friend of the clinic. He's another doctor. He'll be staying in the bedroom over the boathouse for..." He left the last part of the phrase open-ended, giving Ares the chance to set the time-frame.

"Sixty hours or overnight—whichever comes first. Then I'll head for my own place."

Lea smiled. "It looks like you've been on the road for a while."

"You could say that."

"You can give him the cottage, Deakin. I can take the boathouse."

Despite the lines of exhaustion rimming his eyes and mouth, Ares perked up at that. "*You're* the one staying in the cottage?" He shot Deakin a shrewd look.

Oh, don't even go there, bud.

Except he already had, and Lea's face turning a luscious shade of pink wasn't helping any. Was she remembering what they'd done in the cottage the night before?

"I've been staying there, yes."

Deakin was impressed. That cool, efficient tone didn't reflect the color in her face or convey shame or embarrassment. Not that they

had anything to be ashamed of. It was just…
awkward. And he hated that his first sighting
of her this morning had to be in the presence
of someone he knew. Someone who could pick
apart his motivations and memories and twist
them into something they weren't.

Or were they?

"I'm sure there are clean linens ready over
at the boathouse. You know how well Aunt
Cecilia likes to keep things tidy."

"I do. And she'd wrap her apron strings
around my neck if she saw me going in there
and messing it all up."

"Not a chance. She loves you. Probably more
than she loves me."

Ares made a scoffing sound. "Well, much
as I would *love* to keep using the word love,
I'm either going to head over to the boathouse
or I'm going to park myself on the floor of
this clinic and pass out. And I don't think that
would be a cool advertisement for the place."

"Go. I'll see you when you're ready to
emerge from your cocoon. Just knock on the
door of the house. I'll either be there, or here
at the clinic."

One place he would *not* be was at the cottage. Having Ares give him "the look" had
knocked some sense back into him. Clearly his

perceptive friend had picked up on the chemistry between him and Lea.

What did he think he was doing? He and Lea were not headed in the same direction in life. He was on the road or on the way to catch a plane more often than not. And she was looking for a place to land. She'd said it herself.

Theo and Cailey rounded the corner and Deakin could swear that Ares groaned out loud. Then he gave a grunted laugh.

"What the hell *is* this? All we need next is for Petra to come prancing through, doing aerobics."

Since Petra didn't "prance" anywhere, the thought struck Deakin as funny for some reason. He did his best to change his laugh into a cough, just as Theo recognized their friend.

Not that there was any chance he wouldn't. Other islanders might see a vagrant but, as scruffy as he looked, Ares was still Ares. Maybe a little more cynical-sounding than he remembered, but from what he'd heard his friend had been in some pretty tough places.

"Ares!" Theo came forward with a grin and clapped him on the back. "Are you in there somewhere?"

"Oh, funny—you all should have thrown your trust fund money into a comedy club instead of a clinic."

"Or maybe a soup kitchen," Theo said with another grin.

Cailey came forward, arms open to give him a hug, only to have Ares wave her off.

"I am a stinking, dirty mess. Let me get cleaned up before you come anywhere near me."

They talked for a few more minutes, but Ares really did look as if he was about to keel over.

Deakin fished in his pocket for his car keys and pressed them into his friend's hand. "Go. I'll catch a ride with Lea."

He stopped her with a look, knowing she was about to remind him that she'd ridden a bike to work for the past month and a half. And he wasn't about to be her biker babe, riding on the back while she pedaled away. Especially not after last night. Although wrapping his arms around her waist and holding on tight sounded pretty appealing…maybe even letting his hands wander up her belly until they reached…

Ah, hell. He would ask Theo to drive him home. Once Lea had left the building.

He went to pick up Ares's duffle bag, but his friend beat him to it, slinging it over his shoulder like it was nothing, despite eyes that were bloodshot with exhaustion and speech that was beginning to slur.

Slapping him on the back once more, he said, "Call if you need anything, okay?" He paused. "Oh, and Ares…?"

"Yeah?"

"It's good to have you home."

"It's good to be back." He gave a rueful smile. "I *think*. I'll let you know for sure once I'm back in possession of my faculties."

Deakin could understand that sentiment exactly. He'd kind of surprised himself by referring to Mythelios as home, because he hadn't thought of it in those terms for years. Maybe even a decade.

And, as much as he didn't want to admit the reason for that, he had a feeling it was due to the woman standing just a few feet away, observing them with interest.

Was it professional interest or personal? It was something he'd asked himself repeatedly today. She'd slammed that calendar down last night like she really cared. But *did* she? Or had she just been worried, one professional to another, that he was in denial about his old injuries?

And if she did care? Where did that leave him?

He had no idea.

Lea made him want what he couldn't have. What he shouldn't have. And, try as he might, he knew right here and now that it was going to be hard—damned hard—to turn back the hands of time and return to the way his life used to be.

CHAPTER NINE

THE *TAVERNA* WAS already crowded, judging from the cars jamming the parking lot, and Lea had no idea what she was doing there, other than she'd seen Deakin's red Jeep parked out front and had made a quick U-turn, leaving her bike propped against the side of the building.

Seeing Deakin's old friend in the clinic yesterday, and hearing about his radical change in appearance, had made her think about the reasons someone might make such a huge alteration to their physical appearance. Or their personality. It had also made her think of Mark, and the subtle shifts in his behavior that she hadn't noticed at the time but that had made her go back now and pick apart her responses.

Had it made Deakin want to tackle Stavros again? Maybe he was worried that the bartender might harm himself. Or someone else.

He hadn't asked her to come this time, but if she could do anything to help she would.

Pushing open the door and entering the artificially darkened space, she paused to let her eyes adjust to the interior. Stavros was behind the bar, towel flung over his left shoulder, one hand on the polished wooden surface. He was laughing. Laughing hard. His booming voice carrying all the way across the room. No sign of the angry guy from before. That might be a good sign. She would keep her fingers crossed and hope for the best.

She continued scanning the patrons, feeling kind of silly now that she was here.

She saw him. At the other end of the bar from Stavros. His eyes were fastened on her, his jaw tight, and there was some kind of drink in front of him.

Run away. Run away fast.

The internal voice was gradually getting louder and more insistent. But if she left it would look as if she'd run away because of *him.*

And...? Your point is...?

He certainly wasn't waving her over or anything—but, since he was the only one she knew here, and since he didn't appear to have company, she inched her chin up and made her way over to him.

Perching on the empty bar stool next to him, she glanced at his glass and its white contents. He also had a plate of cheese, meats and some other delicious-looking things.

"Ouzo?"

"Yes."

"Is it as strong as they say it is?"

He turned the small glass a couple of times, looking at its contents. "Let's just say it's best not to drink it on an empty stomach." He nodded at the plate of food in front of him. "Compliments of Stavros."

"Compliments? You weren't going to order anything to eat?"

Had he come here to get drunk?

"I was thinking about it."

At first she thought she'd made the comment about getting drunk out loud. But, no. Maybe he was reading her mind. She decided to talk to keep her brain from thinking too much.

She frowned. "How is Stavros? He seems happier today."

"That he does. Would you like something to drink?"

"Actually, I'll have what you're having. I've always wanted to try ouzo. What makes it white?"

He lifted his glass and tilted it slightly. "It's

clear in the bottle, but mix it with water or ice and it turns all…misty."

Just like she was feeling tonight. She wasn't sure what it was, but she felt out of sorts. Kind of itchy and dissatisfied. She had no reason to be. Theo had almost guaranteed she'd be offered a position at the clinic. It was everything she'd hoped for and more. Wasn't it?

He motioned down the bar with an upraised hand. "Stavros? Can I get another of the same?"

The bartender made his way toward them, tossing his towel from one hand to the next, his energy surprising compared to the last time she'd seen him.

"You'd better go easy on those."

"It's not for me. It's for Lea. And if we could have some *calamari* to go with that, we'd appreciate it."

"Sure thing."

Grabbing a bottle from the multi-shelved unit behind him, he twirled it in his hand, getting a glass from under the bar. Then he stopped and seemed to sway for a second. It was over so quickly that Lea almost missed it. Deakin *had* missed it. He'd been busy plucking a piece of cheese from the plate.

Stavros poured the drink over ice with a completely steady hand, no sign that he was even aware of his momentary unsteadiness. Maybe she'd imagined it. She was imagining a whole lot of things these days.

The bartender set the glass on a paper napkin in front of her, keeping his hand on it. "Go easy on her. We've carried more than one tourist out of here after they misjudged her. She did *not* go easy on them."

Being called a tourist stung a little, but since the islanders were a close-knit bunch she could understand it. The funny thing was she felt like a bit of an outsider whether she was in Canada or Greece. She wasn't quite Canadian. And she wasn't quite Greek. She was in some nebulous zone between nationalities. What she was feeling was probably what most immigrants felt from time to time.

Only Mythelios was different. It had felt exactly right from the moment her feet had hit the soil.

"I'll be careful. I may not even finish this one."

"Sip it slowly. Ask Deakin if he'll share his *mezedes* with you until your *calamari* is ready. It should be in about ten minutes."

"Thank you."

Once he was gone, she glanced at Deakin. "Have you noticed anything odd about Stavros tonight?"

"No, he seems to be almost back to normal. If he *has* a normal."

She hesitated, unsure of whether she should even mention what she'd seen. "He does seem better. But when he was getting my drink he stumbled…or swayed, or something."

Deakin looked down the bar to where the bartender was handing one of the kitchen staff their *calamari* order. "Really? I should have been keeping a closer eye on him."

"He was laughing pretty hard at something when I came in, too."

"Was he?" Pushing his plate toward her, he handed her a tiny aperitif fork. "He's right. Don't drink it on an empty stomach. An ouzo hangover is bad news."

She smiled. "And you know this how?"

"Don't ask." He waited until she'd speared one of the small tomatoes on the meat and cheese plate. "I'm surprised you stopped in here. I thought this wasn't one of your favorite places."

She shrugged as nonchalantly as she could, swallowing her bite of food. "It's growing on me. Especially now that I know Stavros isn't normally such a bear."

"No…he isn't." The words had a speculative ring to them and Deakin looked down the bar again. "He does seem closer to normal, but I would agree with you that he still seems a little off—although I missed the unsteadiness you saw."

"Could he have had the flu?"

"Flu doesn't normally cause mood swings."

"You're right."

She picked up her drink and swirled it for a second, then took a tiny sip. It was sweet. And there was something else…

"It tastes like something familiar."

"It has anise in it. Black licorice?"

"Hmm…maybe that's it. It's very good." She took another sip.

He pushed the plate at her yet again. "More food."

This time she chose cheese, which was strong and salty and…*good*. So good. "Mmm. This place is definitely growing on me."

She turned to face him as he took a drink from his own glass, and she noticed he had almost finished his ouzo. One of his fingers reached up to rub at his neck, where the scars were.

"Do they still bother you?"

His hand dropped back to the bar. "No, it's just a habit."

She debated long and hard about asking her next question. It was really none of her business, but she'd *slept* with the man, for heaven's sake. They'd discussed condom use. Surely she was entitled to know a few things about his personal life.

"You said you got them during a fire. Was it at home?"

The smoke alarms told her it had been. Or at least that it had been at a place he hadn't expected to get burned.

Another sip of his ouzo went down. So far she'd only seen him eat one piece from the *mezedes* plate.

"Yes. At home. In my father's boathouse, actually."

"The one where your friend spent last night?"

"No, it was a different boathouse. My dad rebuilt it. And bought a new boat."

Okay, so she was right. The fire *hadn't* been some small, strike-a-match kiddie fire. It had been big. Big enough to cause the extensive tissue destruction she'd seen across his chest.

"What happened?"

His brows went up as another sip went down. "I decided to try smoking for the first time." He gave a humorless laugh. "Let's just say it was an explosive experience."

"The boathouse *exploded*? God! How old were you?"

"Yes. Gas fumes and matches don't play well together. I was fourteen at the time."

"Oh, Deakin. You could have been killed."

"Hmm..."

The way he'd said that... It almost sounded as if he'd *wanted* to be killed.

"Did you set the fire on purpose?" Kids younger than he'd been committed suicide far too often.

"What?" His brows slammed together. "God, no. What made you think that?"

Okay, she hadn't meant to make him angry.

Stavros came and set down the calamari, and then went off to take care of other customers. She was beginning to think she should have kept her wonderings to herself.

"I don't know. I was just asking. A lot of kids play with fire. It's kind of a rite of passage."

"Well, believe me, this was no rite of passage. And, since I almost took out another kid in the process, I'd say I got everything I deserved. I'm sure plenty of folks in Mythelios think the same thing."

Stavros had made a crack about Deakin's father the first time they'd come in here. Had that been in reference to the fire?

"I doubt that. It was a long time ago. I bet most people have probably forgotten."

"Maybe they have. But *I* haven't. My dad was taken to the police station and questioned after it happened. I didn't find out about that until I was in medical school. And my friend Ville got in huge trouble with his parents. They beat him. Broke his arm. Even though he'd been burned as well."

"How terrible. What did the police do?"

"To my dad? Or to Ville's dad?"

"Ville's, of course."

"Nothing. Ville claimed it had happened in the explosion. No one doubted him."

"I'm *so* sorry." She took another bracing drink.

Was that why Deakin stayed away from the island so much? Because he thought people would throw the past back in his face?

"Like everyone keeps saying…it happened a long time ago." He downed the last of his drink. "Eat your octopus."

That sounded like an order. And Lea didn't take orders very well.

"Would you like to try that again? Especially since *you've* eaten almost nothing and finished your drink in less than twenty minutes."

Deakin's half-smile appeared. "Eat your octopus. *Please*."

He was incorrigible. But appealing.

She picked up one of the fried treats and bit

it in half. The crispy coating was delicately seasoned so it didn't overpower the seafood inside. "Oh, this is delicious."

"Stavros has always done a good job with *mezedes*."

"You're not kidding. Try some."

"I'm okay."

He didn't order another drink, which she was glad of. She certainly didn't want him driving if he was tipsy. And she could very easily see how it could happen with this drink. The sugar in the alcohol would keep it from getting released into the system as quickly as it might otherwise. But once it did… Well, you certainly wouldn't want to be driving home.

She popped another delicious piece of calamari into her mouth. "Did *your* dad give you a hard time about the boathouse?" she asked once she'd finished.

He gave a pained grunt. "You mean did he beat me? No. I think my skin grafts and surgeries did that for him. He actually never said a word about it. Just rebuilt his boathouse. And then replaced his beloved boat."

"That's the boat you use now?"

"One and the same."

"I'm sorry that happened to you and your friend." She slid her hand over his wrist, trying to give him a little bit of support.

His eyes came up and speared hers. "Feeling sorry for me now?"

"No. But I think it's time to stop beating yourself up for something that happened years ago." She leaned her head against his shoulder, the act feeling as right as the island did. "And if someone tries to dig up the past just tell them to bugger off."

He laughed, his right hand sliding over her cheek and moving to her nape, his thumb strumming a tune on her jawline. "You surprise me—you know that?"

"I do?"

Each light stroke along her skin sent frissons of awareness spiraling through her belly, the circles slowing spreading outward.

"You do. Every time I think I have you figured out…"

His words trailed off, but the caresses said that he was busy thinking of other things right now. At least she hoped he was.

The hand at her nape moved to her chin, tilting it so he could look at her. "I want to get out of here."

She lowered her voice to a whisper. "I want that too."

That was evidently all he needed to hear, because he dug his wallet out of his pants pocket and peeled off a couple of bills. More than what their drinks and appetizers were worth, she was sure. But he dropped the money on the bar, flashed a signal at Stavros for good effect. The other man noticed it and nodded in their direction.

Then Deakin was towing her out of the bar and heading toward his car.

"My bike. It's parked against the wall."

"We'll throw it in the back of the Jeep."

"Are you okay to drive?"

"Yes. I know my limits."

Did he? Well, he was doing better than she was—because she thought the sips of ouzo she'd had were swirling around in her head and messing with her common sense. She hadn't eaten nearly enough to counter the effects.

He picked her bike up with one hand and tossed it into the back of the Jeep. He then unlocked the passenger side door and pulled it open.

"Where are we going?"

Leaning down, he whispered in her ear. "Does it matter?"

"No…" It didn't matter. All she knew was that she wanted to go with him no matter where he wanted to be.

They made it back to his place and Deakin slid the gearshift into "park" before leaning over and kissing her, his lips pressed to hers in a way that had her heart pounding.

Her body was well aware of where this was headed. It had known ever since she'd sat on that bar stool and asked him to tell her about the fire. He had. And it was pretty obvious that he didn't tell that story to many people. Yes, they might know the bitter facts about what had happened, but Deakin had *lived* it. And it made her sad. And mad. And, *oh*, so sorry for the two teenagers who had paid such an awful price for being curious.

When Deakin climbed out of the car she noticed he hadn't parked it next to the house or the cottage. It was beside the boathouse instead.

A flutter rippled through her tummy. She scrambled out of the car and onto the sidewalk. "Are we going boating?"

It was already dark, even though the sun hadn't been down long. "We are. Are you game?"

Yes. She was. She trusted him—could tell that while the alcohol might have pried a few secrets out of him it hadn't incapacitated him as far as driving went.

He stopped just inside the dark building. "I want to make love to you. On the boat."

Her throat went dry at the hint of wistful

longing she heard in his voice. She turned toward him and slid her fingers deep into the hair at his nape, sighing as his scent washed over her. Rough and masculine, it drove her crazy. *He* drove her crazy.

"I want that too."

His hands went to her hips and he yanked her against him. He was already hard, the edge of his erection pressing into her belly. Holding her there, he lowered his head and captured her lips, his tongue delving in and testing the waters. His mouth was doing what she wanted other parts of him to be doing.

She tugged back. "Boat."

"Your wish…"

Scooping her up, he carried her inside the boathouse and down the plank decking toward where the vessel was moored.

"I can walk."

He didn't set her down. "So can I."

And he could, stepping across the small space between the dock and the boat with ease.

Once aboard, he did set her down, giving her another quick kiss. "Just let me untie and get it ready."

What? She didn't want him to get anything ready but her. "I thought we were just going to stay here."

"Oh, no, *agape mou.* That would be like

necking in a car that's parked in a garage. There's no thrill in that."

There was *plenty* of thrill in that. At least in *her* estimation. But she could at least make leaving the boathouse a little more difficult for him.

Walking up behind him, where he was untying the rope from one of the cleats, she wrapped her arms around his waist and pressed herself against him. Her hands slid down his flat abs and ducked below the waistband of his jeans—only to have him grab them and wrap them around his midsection instead.

"Last time you got me too hot and bothered too fast. Not this time."

"I seem to remember that you made up for that as the night went on."

Gripping one of her wrists, he turned around and then pressed it against the hard bulge in his jeans. "This is saying, *Hurry, hurry.* You need to help me say, *Slow down...*"

"But what if I don't *want* to slow down? What if I want the car in the garage?"

He chuckled, pressing her even tighter against him. "That was the wrong analogy to make, because right now I'm having a hard time thinking about anything except driving the car into the garage."

It took her a minute to get his meaning,

and then her eyes widened. "Then what are we waiting for? Let's pull the boat out of its boathouse and put it wherever you want it."

"Wherever I want it? Because boats and cars are all very sexy words right now…" He dropped her hand. "Why don't you go below and check out the bed while I get us underway."

She did as he asked, going down the four steps, moving through the kitchen to where she knew the small bedroom was. She pushed through the door and looked at the bed. What was she supposed to do with it now that she was here?

Ah… She had seen the perfect thing.

Deakin dropped anchor about two miles offshore. There they would be free of anyone possibly coming by—like Ares. His friend had already packed up and gone home after a long, much-needed sleep, but if he'd forgotten something Deakin would have hated for him to walk in on them in the boathouse. Plus the time on the water had given him a chance to cool his body down.

The second she'd wrapped her arms around him he'd been ready to throw her on the deck and have her right there. But he didn't want a rushed affair this time. He wanted it to last.

Wanted to actually taste and savor, much like he'd done with the ouzo. No tossing back a couple of shots and calling it a day.

You could learn a lot from the famous Greek drink. Like how to take it slow even when everything inside you was telling you just to chug it quick.

He got up from his seat and stretched, surprised that Lea hadn't come up from below yet. He'd meant for her to check and make sure there were clean sheets on the bed—something he wasn't sure if his aunt would have taken care of like she did the beds in the other residences.

Where *was* she?

Only one way to find out.

He put his hand on the door post and ducked under the low ceiling as he went down the steps. "Lea?"

"In here."

Well, he could have figured *that* out—unless she'd jumped overboard. Actually, maybe she would be smarter to abandon ship than to stay. But she'd asked about his accident in such a matter-of-fact voice. There had been no condemnation in her tones, no horror or shock at what he'd done. Then again, she hadn't flinched at all when she'd seen his chest.

The door to the bedroom was closed.

He frowned. "Everything okay in there?"

"Yes. Come on in."

He opened the door and went inside—and then his body went icy cold. There were candles lit everywhere, including on the bed, where Lea lay on her back, completely naked, a thick squat candle seated in the curve of her belly.

"Put them out. *Right now.*" His voice shook and bile washed up his throat.

Lea sat up in a hurry, setting the candle aside and getting on her knees. She grabbed his hands. "Deakin, they're not real. They're battery-operated. I'm so sorry. I didn't think they looked so realistic, that you might think…"

He *had* thought it, and his abject terror of those things catching everything down here on fire had put out the blaze inside him that he'd been so worried about.

He sank onto the bed, elbows on his knees, hands supporting his chin. "It's okay. I should have realized my father would never have allowed real candles on the boat."

Now that the fear was trickling away he glanced around and saw about ten of the same kind of *faux* candles. He picked up the one in the middle of the bed and rattled it inside its faceted container. It cast a soft, muted light around the room, and his and Lea's shadows appeared enormous on the far wall.

She came up behind him and put her hands on his shoulders, squeezed the tense muscles there, her fingers moving along each row with sure, firm strokes.

His eyes closed as she continued to work her magic, across his shoulder blades and then down his spine. "Feels good…"

"I'm glad." Her lips touched his earlobe. "I'm very sorry for scaring you."

"Not very manly of me, I know."

This time she gently bit his ear. "I can't think of anyone more manly than you."

And that did the trick. The flesh that had receded began to unfurl again, becoming tense and firm. This was one muscle he *didn't* want the tension worked out of. Well, he did. But in a completely different way.

Her ministering hands moved from his shoulders and slid over his chest. A button popped free from his shirt. Then another. It was then that he remembered she'd been naked when he'd walked into this room. Was still naked even now.

He captured her hands and carried one of them to his mouth. "It seems like you always have all the fun." He glanced around the room at the flickering of a dozen artificial wicks.

"And I *like* your candles. Thank you for thinking of them."

Standing to his feet, he turned and looked at her. She was on her knees in the middle of the bed, her breasts bare, her belly with its indented waist appearing golden in the low light. He wanted to explore that play of light a little bit more. But first he needed to take the edge off. And since the edge was those wandering hands he needed to do something about them. But what?

"Stay right there for a minute."

"What?"

He slid his hands in between her calves and her knees and tugged hard, tipping her onto her back in an instant. He glanced down and saw his solution. His shirt. He stripped it off and shook out the long sleeves, gripping them and then flipping the main part of the shirt over and over until it formed a kind of rope.

"Do you trust me?"

"Yes."

"Then give me your hands."

Her eyes widened as she realized what he wanted to do. "You have a *bad* side to you..." She put her hands together and held them toward him.

"Do I?"

"I'm thinking yes. But what's good for the goose... I *do* get to reciprocate later, right?"

The thought of her tying him up and running those skillful fingers all over his body made him break out in a cold sweat. To combat the sensation he wound the shirt around her hands and tied it snugly enough that she would have to struggle to get loose. Then he put her arms over her head. Well away from any of his danger zones.

"We can negotiate those terms later on. Right now it's about you lying as still as you can. And letting me do anything I want to you."

CHAPTER TEN

THEY'D STAYED ON the boat all night. And Lea *had* reciprocated.

Deakin had loved every minute of it. Hadn't been able to wait to have her all over again.

He'd slept with other women, and although they'd expressed the same curiosity Lea had about his scars, he'd never opened up to any of them. And in the morning, when he'd parked the boat in its little slip, she'd kissed the back of his neck and told him she needed to go change for work. As if the night they'd shared had been nothing out of the ordinary for her.

Well, it had been for him.

He'd let her go because he hadn't been sure what to do with the swirl of emotions that was making a mess of everything.

She seemed to care about him. In fact she was much less stressed about all this than he was. She just took everything in her stride in that calm way of hers.

So where did they go from here? She was officially still between jobs. Would she be willing to travel the world with him? To see if things between them kept on sizzling like they were now?

And if they did?

Maybe then he'd be willing to take it to the next level.

Say yes to a relationship?

Maybe.

The question was, would she leave the island? For him? For them?

He had no idea. What he *did* know was that he needed to get to work and worry about his personal life later.

The clinic's boardroom wasn't big. Then again, neither was the board of directors. Theo had called them in for a meeting about Lea. Deakin waited, a little impatient about this whole production. His friend had already told him that they wanted to pay Lea for her time and he'd already agreed to it. But, since Theo was the one holding down the fort while the rest of them worked elsewhere, he took advantage of the times they *were* here to take care of business. Which meant they would have to vote on it as a group.

Ares and Theo arrived together, laughing

about something. The two of them took seats across from Deakin, then Theo opened up his laptop and punched some keys.

"Just calling Chris. I told him that we'd be meeting, and he arranged his schedule so he could join us via online chat."

Okay… Deakin still didn't understand what the big deal was, but he was fine with it. He'd attended few enough of these meetings over the years. And, really, he was grateful for how much time and effort Theo put in to keeping this place running.

Within minutes his friend had the other member of the board on the line. "Hi, Chris, can you hear us?" he asked.

Chris replied in the affirmative.

"Well, let's get down to business. The clinic is running short of funds, due to the earthquake, and the CT scanner isn't working at the moment—so we have expenses coming out the wazoo and no way to pay them. Which is why the bachelor auction will help supplement the money the calendar has already brought in."

That damned calendar. Deakin would be more than glad when July was over.

Chris's voice came through. "I'll do what I can once I get there."

It was then that Deakin noticed Ares was staring fixedly at a spot on the table. Maybe he was as bored as Deakin was. It seemed like the meeting was going on for ages, with them just voting through item after item, like they usually did.

"Last on our agenda is a vote to add a new staff position to our roster."

Last? What had happened to paying Lea for the services she'd been providing ever since the earthquake had hit the island? It wasn't like Theo to forget something like that. But with a baby coming it was understandable that his thoughts might be centered on his unborn child and his fiancée. He would remind Theo of their conversation once he was done talking.

"I've already talked to both Lea and Deakin and they've agreed."

Lea? Why was Theo asking her about adding a staff position? Unless it was to get her professional feedback as they went through the search process?

He hoped she might not be around on the island long enough to be of any assistance. He hadn't talked to her yet about coming with him on his next assignment, but he was planning to. Either today or tomorrow. All he could hope was that she didn't get spooked and take off before he had a chance to explain his thoughts.

"So let's put it to a vote. All those in favor of adding Lea Risi to our permanent staff, say yes."

Chris said yes before Deakin's shocked brain even had a chance to process what had just been said.

Lea was the new staff member?

And she hadn't said a word to him about it?

A throbbing set up in his left temple, the dull ache gaining traction with each second that passed.

"Wait a minute." He held up a hand. "That's not what you and I talked about the other day, Theo. You said something about *paying* her, not hiring her."

"No, I asked if you thought she was a valuable addition to the clinic."

He *had* asked that. But at the time Deakin had assumed Theo was speaking about temporary hired help. Not in terms of a permanent position.

Had Lea already agreed to this?

"I didn't fully understand what you were suggesting."

Theo waited a beat, then continued. "That's okay. Now that I've made it a little clearer, what do you say?"

"I say no."

The words were out of his mouth before he

had a chance to really think about them. Ten seconds later the room erupted, with everyone speaking at once.

Theo stood and stared them into silence. "You agreed that she was good for the clinic and that people loved her. *And* that she should be paid for her services. I have no idea why you wouldn't welcome her with open arms."

He already had. But if they voted her in it meant she couldn't go with him when he left. Unless she turned them down.

Was he willing to take that chance?

And why was he so adamantly opposed to the job being offered to her?

He searched his heart. Dug deep and really examined his motives. The events of last night and the previous days played in his mind, the tape running over and over again.

Hell. He knew why. Knew why he'd voted no. Knew why he'd been so anxious to corner her about joining his relief organization.

He loved her.

It wasn't about seeing if the spark in their relationship stayed or whether they could get along outside the bedroom. He wanted her with him because he was already head over heels for her.

That was why he'd voted no.

They all needed to take a breath until he

could get to Lea and talk to her. Tell her what he was thinking.

The solution came to him in an instant—and he was going to exploit Theo's own words.

"I don't think we can afford a new staff member at the moment. You said it yourself. The clinic is operating within very narrow margins. We're having to do additional fundraisers to cover the shortfall. And now we're going to hire another doctor? I'm sorry, but I just don't think this is the right time to be making changes like that."

His chest tightened. He knew he was running roughshod over people he cared about very much. He couldn't care less if they hired *ten* new people, as long as one of them wasn't Lea.

Theo's face was tight with anger, but to his credit he didn't explode. "Well, I guess that settles it, then. We've always voted for things unanimously, although in this case I wish we hadn't established that precedent." He looked at Deakin and raised an eyebrow. "Any chance we can convince you to change your vote?"

"Not at this time."

If Lea decided that this was what she wanted—to stay on Mythelios permanently—then he would give her his blessing and catch the next flight out of here. But until he heard the words come out of her mouth he was going to give this a chance to take off.

None of his friends seemed to understand his reasoning any better than Theo did, but they finished up and let Chris go back to what he needed to be doing.

Ares just shook his head and left the room.

Theo stayed a moment longer, giving him a long, hard look. "I'm really disappointed, Deak. I'd hoped for better from you." Then he too walked out.

Deakin slowly sat down in his chair and let out a huge breath. He would make it up to his friends. At least he hoped he would. Once Lea had agreed to continue their relationship, hopefully they would all understand why he'd voted the way he had, and why he'd been so anxious to keep them from talking her into staying.

And if he talked to her and she wanted to stay on Mythelios?

Well, he was leaving.

With Lea or without her.

In the end, the choice was up to her.

"Why don't you want me working at the clinic?"

Lea did her best to keep the hurt from showing in her voice, but it was useless. Everything inside her was shaking. Including her voice.

She hadn't believed it when Theo told her Deakin had cast the only dissenting vote, but the look on the other doctor's face had said it all. He was serious. Deakin had voted against her.

His features went blank. "Theo told you?"

"Of course he did. Did you think he wouldn't?"

Her eyes burned in her head, but she refused to give in to the tears. Not yet. Not when she had so much to get off her chest.

She'd trusted this man. Had grown to care about him. And then he'd turned around and stabbed her in the back? *Why?*

"I'd hoped to be able to talk to you before you found out."

"And exactly what were you going to say to me?"

"I was hoping you wouldn't want to stay."

A fresh stab of hurt pierced her heart. She'd held a modicum of hope that Theo might have misunderstood Deakin, that she could bring Deakin to her office and clear this up. She hadn't needed to look for him, though. Deakin had come to her instead.

Thankfully there were no patients around to overhear their little exchange.

"Well, that's pretty damned obvious, don't you think? The thing is, I *did* want to stay. I love this island, and when Theo mentioned

the possibility of a permanent position here…
Well, I was thrilled, frankly."

"You were?"

"Of course I was. Theo said he'd already
spoken to you about it and that you were in
favor. So I just don't understand the change
in your attitude…"

It went deeper than that. She'd told him on
the boat that she trusted him. And she had.
She'd trusted him with her life. Her wellbe-
ing. To find out she'd made a mistake was the
worst kind of betrayal.

"I just don't think we should make any rash
decisions," he said.

His tanned features had paled. His mouth
looked pinched and white. Probably guilt over
what he'd done.

"*Rash?* Seems like you've made plenty of
rash decisions over the last couple of weeks."

He'd been quick enough to jump into bed
with her. What was that if not rash? And *she'd*
been rash enough to—

Oh, hell. No.

She was in *love* with him? No way. Not after
what he'd just done.

But the tug in her heart remained, the tearing sensation inside of her going deep. And it
hurt. God, it hurt so badly.

"You seriously want to stay? On the island?" he asked.

"Yes. I seriously do."

And she had seriously hoped that Deakin might want to stay on the island with her. Well, that hope was shot to hell now. If he was staying, she was going.

Hadn't she sworn off baggage-carrying men? Well, it looked like she had just picked out another one. But this time she was going to send him spinning away before things got out of hand.

Good grief, Lea. They're already way out of hand.

But she couldn't deal with this. Not right now.

Looking back, she should have seen the signs. If someone had stood outside the *taverna* and held up a neon sign they couldn't have made the message any more plain: He despised his scars. He'd installed the biggest, baddest fire alarms known to man and freaked out whenever one of them made a peep. Like at burned eggs. He flipped out over fake candles. Instead of really looking at them—trusting her not to make a stupid decision—he'd just reacted. Like he'd done over every other thing since she'd known him.

And the *pièce de resistance* was his knee jerk reaction now, to the clinic hiring her.

Well, that was the last decision he would ever make regarding her.

"We've had a lot of fun over the last couple of weeks. And if any of it meant anything I'm going to ask you to do one thing for me." She leaned forward. "I'm going to ask you to change your vote."

"And if I say no?"

"Then I'll leave. But it won't be without a fight."

"Why do you want to stay so much, Lea?"

She could see the confusion on his face, hear it in his voice. She didn't know how to make him understand how she felt about the island and wasn't sure she should even try. But she had to.

"Just because this island doesn't mean anything to you, it doesn't mean it can't to someone else. I love it here. I want to stay."

This time her voice didn't shake. It was calm and clear and filled with all the sincerity she could muster.

A muscle worked in his jaw. "You're absolutely sure?"

"Never more sure of anything in my life."

He stood to his feet and stared down at her, something hard and decisive appearing in his gaze before he blinked it away. "You have my vote, then. I'll tell Theo."

He didn't try to get her to change her mind. Didn't explain his reasoning or ask to talk things through. A wave of uncertainty went through her, but it was too late to take back the words, so she simply said, "Thank you. You won't regret this."

No other hint of emotion flickered through his eyes. "That's where you're wrong, Lea. Because I already do."

Then he turned on his heel and walked away.

When he was out of sight she sagged in her seat and laid her head on her desk as bitter tears splashed onto the wooden surface.

She had a feeling that in winning the battle she'd just lost the most important war ever.

CHAPTER ELEVEN

THE FIRST WEEK off the island had been the worst.

Deakin had sat in a bar in Athens and drunk himself into a stupor the first two nights. He'd spent the rest of his days trying to pull himself up by his bootstraps.

It was over. Lea had made her decision and he'd made his.

Right—like boozing it up with strangers who don't give a damn about you?

Broken bits of the past three weeks ran through his head, brushing against the damaged parts of his being and making him look at things in a new way.

Mythelios held so many terrible memories for him, but was that really the island's fault? No. It was his.

His first day back he'd shaken hands with several locals who'd murmured how good it was that he'd come home—and they'd meant it. There were people he loved there—Theo, Cailey, Ares, Chris, Petra, his Aunt Cecilia, to name a few. And they loved him in return. They cared about him despite his stupidity as a kid. They looked past his scars and saw the same Deakin they'd always seen. Their friend. Relative. Partner.

Even Stavros had apologized for his outburst about his dad the night he'd gone in to binge on ouzo—before Lea had come waltzing in and made him want her all over again.

He never had got to talk to her about leaving the island with him. Because she'd been dead set on staying, and so very angry about what he'd done. And rightly so. He'd had no right to take that decision out of her hands, no matter what his reasons.

In the end it had changed nothing. She'd stayed. And he'd left.

Her final words to him had haunted him: *"You won't regret it."*

How the hell would he *not* regret it? The woman he loved had chosen an island over him.

But had she? Had she really? he wondered. Or had he forced her into a decision she hadn't wanted to make?

No, he'd tried to force her into the decision

he wanted her to make. And in doing so he'd sealed his own fate.

They couldn't have carried on a relationship from different areas of the globe even if she felt something for him. Had he imagined all of that? The way her hands had massaged his fear away when he'd discovered those candles on the boat. The way she'd kissed his scars. The way she had quietly asked what had happened to him. And all the time her eyes had been soft with understanding. Caring…?

Was that why he'd been able to see the devastation on her face when she'd realized he was the one who'd voted against her? He could understand her anger. But there'd also been a deep hurt behind those green eyes. A pain that rivaled his own.

So what should he do now? Fly off and move on to his next assignment? Or go back to the island and see if he could face down the demons of his own making and banish them? For good, this time.

Then he could sit down and talk to Lea. Get everything he'd wanted to say earlier off his chest. Even if she rejected him outright he would know once and for all.

As it was, the doubts were eating at his soul one glass of ouzo at a time. Soon there'd be nothing left.

Unless he did something about it.

Today.

And maybe that something should begin with a phone call to someone from his past. Someone he'd never quite made his peace with. Maybe then he could finally slam that door on all the painful memories and lock it tight. Once and for all.

They had a gardener who weeded the Serenity Gardens. But right now it was the only thing Lea wanted to do. It was her day off, but the thought of going back to that cottage, knowing the house next door was empty, probably for good, was just too depressing.

She'd gone to talk to Deakin the day after their confrontation in her office, hoping to understand why he'd done what he had, but it had been too late. He was gone.

He hadn't thought she'd want to stay? Why? Hadn't she shown how much she loved everything about Mythelios?

Including Deakin?

Except Deakin didn't love the island. She realized that the day they went to Delos. The change in him had been dramatic.

Her grief over Mark had made her wary of trusting her judgment again. So she'd painted

Deakin with Mark's brush and decided he was just too damaged to take a chance on.

But the whole idea of her job was that there was hope for everyone. As long as they were willing to work to improve their situation.

Was she willing to improve hers?

She'd thought she was doing just that, but now she wondered.

The heat beat down on her and she pushed her hat a little further forward on her head, another pang going through her. This was the same hat she'd worn on their Delos excursion. The first time she'd thought he might be as attracted to her as she was to him.

So why had he voted against her?

"I didn't think you wanted to stay."

So where did he think she wanted to go?

There was no answer to that question. She yanked another weed out and placed it on the growing pile beside her. She wasn't absolutely positive they were all weeds, but each tug released a little bit of the destructive anger and frustration she'd allowed to build inside her.

Where did he think she wanted to go?

That last night on his boat had been a magical experience. He'd made love to her like no man ever had. Not even Mark. A mixture of sexy urgency melded with slow, thorough loving. Different and yet the same.

So what was she supposed to do now? He'd left and she had no idea where he'd gone.

She could call his NGO. Except she wasn't really sure of the name of the organization.

Wasn't that just beating around the bush, though? She had his cellphone number. Why not just call him?

And have to listen to his voice as he told her he didn't love her?

Yes. Why not? At least then she'd know one way or the other and could move forward with her life.

Sliding her gloves off her hands, she reached into her pocket and pulled out her cellphone. She scrolled through the numbers until she came across one that was all too familiar. The question was, did she have the courage to call him?

If he didn't want to talk to her he would probably just let it go to voicemail. And then she'd still have her answer.

Just do it, Lea.

Before she could talk herself out of it she pushed the button. Her heart pounded in her chest, her mouth suddenly going dry. She wasn't sure she'd be able to talk even if he did answer.

There. It was ringing.

In the garden another person's phone began

to ring. She glanced around, not wanting to have a conversation like this when someone else was in the area.

A shadow appeared on the ground next to her. The ringing phone was linked with who-ever it was.

"Hello?"

Oh, God. That voice. He could be right here in the room with her it was so clear.

"Deakin?"

Someone crouched next to her and suddenly the voice on the phone was right in her ear.

"I'm right here."

She dropped the phone, turning in a rush to find herself face to face with the very man she'd been thinking about.

"You're *here*!"

He smiled. "Yes." He picked up the trowel beside her. "Is this one of your duties as the new staff member? Theo told me they hired you. Congratulations."

"Thank you."

She swallowed, searching for words that wouldn't be meaningless. He might only be here between flights or something. In fact this might be the last time she would ever see him, so she needed to make every second count.

He stood to his feet and reached down a hand. She let him pull her up, memorizing the feel of her palm in his. A slash of pain went through her. She didn't want him to go.

"Why did you vote the way you did?"

"It's complicated."

"We're *all* complicated, Deakin, and sometimes we need to break things down into simpler parts. You said you didn't think I wanted to stay here. Why?"

He blew out a breath. "I phrased that badly. What I should have said was that I was *hoping* you didn't want to stay."

"Why?"

She realized he hadn't let go of her hand. And she hadn't let go of his.

"I wanted you to come with me instead. To see if we could make what we had work."

A tiny seed of hope rolled around inside her. "And what *did* we have?"

"A chance for a future together." He lifted her hand to his lips and kissed it. "You want simple? Okay. Here it is. I love you."

"What?"

"A complicated compound broken down into its simplest form: Three words. I. Love. You."

"But you voted against me getting a permanent job here. You can't imagine how crushed I was when Theo told me that."

"I know—and I'm sorry. At the time I thought I was voting for *us*. Things in the meeting happened so fast, and I didn't think through the ramifications. Kind of like the night I lit that cigarette and blew my world apart."

"But you never told me any of this."

He smiled. "I never had the chance. Because Theo sideswiped me into doing something incredibly stupid. And then, when I came to see you to try and figure things out, you already knew about the meeting. I know how much you love Mythelios. I've done some serious soul-searching over the last week, and I think if I look at it through your eyes I might come to love it again too. But I'm only willing to do that if you think we have a future together."

A single leaf sprang out of that seed inside of her. "Simplest form?"

"Simplest form."

She swallowed her fear and gave it to him straight. "I love you too."

He tipped back her hat and looked into her face. "I never thought I'd hear those words from you—I thought I'd ruined everything."

Lea traced one of the scars on his neck. "You just fixed it. Thank you for coming back."

"I couldn't leave things the way they were between us."

"Neither could I. I was just trying to call you."

He smiled and planted a kiss on the tip of her nose. "What were you going to say?"

"I don't know. I only know I couldn't bear the thought of you never knowing how I truly feel about you." She went into his embrace, leaning her head against his chest. "And now here you are."

"I couldn't stay away. The *where* doesn't matter as long as I have the right *who*."

"I agree. We don't have to decide everything right now. I just want to sit here beside you and hear you say you love me again and again."

"I'll say it as often as you want. Every day. Every hour. Every minute."

"Oh, wait!"

His brows came together. "What is it?"

"Does this mean I have to bid on you at the auction?"

"No. And do you know why?"

She let him draw her close, not caring who might or might not walk in on them. "Why?"

"Because you won me—" he kissed her "—on that very first day, when you swatted my hand off that patient sign-in list. And now you're stuck with me. Here on this island. Or wherever we might choose to go."

"Shall we get a map and pick a location?"

His hands splayed across the small of her back, the heat of his touch setting off a tingle that was impossible to ignore.

"I don't think a map will be necessary for

the place I want to take you." He traced a path up the middle of her spine. "All we need is you and me to make any place in this world perfect."

EPILOGUE

THE BOTTLE OF champagne struck the side of the vessel with a solid *thunk*, spraying golden bubbles and laughter in all directions.

"Isn't it bad luck to rechristen a boat?"

Lea gripped Deakin's hand, as if she were afraid the past month had been a dream. It hadn't. It was very real. And his fingers tightened around hers, trying to reassure her of that fact.

"No. It's a metamorphosis. A rebirth."

Kind of like Deakin's new lease on life.

"Well, I certainly like *Mythelios Rescue* better than its old name."

After his talk with Ville last month Deakin had made his peace with the past. Donating his father's boat to the clinic had been the final piece in that puzzle.

He and Lea had decided to stay on Mythelios—but it was an open-ended arrangement. Lea was willing to move. And Deakin was willing to stay. He'd opened his heart and suddenly the possibilities were endless.

They were in the process of redecorating his parents' house—another metamorphosis that was long overdue—and his aunt was helping them to turn the place into an actual home. For now they were shacked up in the little cottage. Where Lea cooked eggs with care. And where they loved long into the night.

He'd been right about life being perfect as long as he and Lea were together.

Theo got up and addressed the gathered crowd, starting by thanking Deakin for his generous donation.

"Now, take a good look around, ladies. We have a bachelor auction coming up. Unfortunately our single men seem to be dropping like flies around here."

Laughter rippled across the crowd, before Theo motioned that he wasn't done.

"Our very own Dr. Deakin Patera is now off the market and on his way to wedded bliss. So let's wish them well."

Clapping erupted in the Serenity Gardens, and the *Mythelios Rescue* nodded its approval from its new boat slip.

Deakin wrapped his arms around his fiancée's waist and smiled. "I love you."

"Love you too."

Then he kissed her, and everything else faded away.

Because it was Deakin and Lea in the most perfect place on earth.

* * * * *

Look out for the previous story in the
HOT GREEK DOCS *quartet*

ONE NIGHT WITH DR. NIKOLAIDES
by Annie O'Neil

And there are two more fabulous
stories to come!
Available July 2018!

If you enjoyed this story, check out these
other great reads from Tina Beckett

THE DOCTORS' BABY MIRACLE
THE DOCTOR'S FORBIDDEN
TEMPTATION

Available now!